Jazz Country

Jazz Country

by

Nat Hentoff

Harper & Row, Publishers
New York, Evanston, and London

Standard Book Number 06-022305-7 (Trade Edition)
Standard Book Number 06-022306-5 (Harpercrest Edition)
Library of Congress Catalog Card Number: 65-15557

For Charles Mingus
and for my son, Thomas

Contents

Jazz Country

1
The Outsiders

Mike and I were supposed to go to the movies, but I talked him into coming downtown to the Savoy where Moses Godfrey was playing. We couldn't go inside because they were very careful about letting anyone in who was underage. I know. I'd tried a few months before and this big guy behind the bar had blocked me at the door. "Sonny," he said, "I don't care what kind of identification you've got. A cop gets one look at you inside and I'm suspended for a month." He started to walk away, and then he suddenly turned. "What age *are* you?"

He caught me by surprise. "Sixteen," I said, before I realized I could have at least made a *try.*

"I'll see you in two years." He laughed and went back behind the bar. I felt like I was ten.

Even though Mike and I couldn't go in, we could at least hang around awhile outside, hear some of the music, and get a look at the musicians when they came out between sets. Mike didn't mind because, although he didn't play anything himself, he had a lot of records and he was almost as hung on jazz as I was.

So this night we got there about ten o'clock. It

1

was an especially warm May night, the door was open, and we heard almost a whole set by Godfrey.

"You going to try to talk to him when he gets out?" Mike asked me. Godfrey was supposed to be strange. One of the jazz writers had called him "the mysterious Moses," and the tag had stuck. I'd read that he never gave interviews because he figured his music said all he wanted to say. And if you didn't understand the music, there was no sense *at all* in talking to him.

Godfrey also looked funny. In his early forties, he looked at least fifty. He had a big, round head with a full beard, on a short, stubby body. *Down Beat* said Godfrey always wore dark glasses, even at night inside a club. Another thing about him was that you never knew when he was going to get up and dance. I mean, he'd be playing a solo and then get up from the piano and start dancing. All by himself. And the other guys would keep playing as if nothing unusual was going on. I'd seen him do that once at a concert at Philharmonic Hall. He danced like his music sounded. All angles and surprises. In fact, I guess that's what he was doing. Making his body into an instrument too.

As I was thinking about him, Godfrey came out of the Savoy, leaned against the window, and lit a cigarette. Bill Hitchcock, his bass player, was with him. Hitchcock was only about five years older than I was, but he was already high up on the jazz polls. He was tall and thin and held himself very straight.

I went up to them. "It sure sounded good, Mr. Godfrey." Godfrey looked at me and he kept on looking at me, but he didn't say a word.

I had to find something to say. "Are you going to have a new album out soon?"

"When is soon?" Godfrey said. His voice surprised me. It was soft and high. I'd expected he'd sound like a bear. "Soon." He said it again, slowly. "If I told you," he said to Hitchcock, "your arm would fall off next year, would that be soon?"

Hitchcock smiled. "Too soon. Much too soon."

"But if I told you there'd be no money this week. Maybe soon, but not this week, Would that be soon enough?"

Hitchcock laughed. "Soon enough to bring you up before the union."

"You see?" Godfrey looked at me. "You didn't make yourself clear. What is soon to you might not be soon to me. And the other way around."

I didn't know what to say because I wasn't sure if he was putting me on or if he always talked that way.

Mike, who had just been standing there with his mouth open, came alive. "I've got all your LP's, Mr.

Godfrey." Godfrey made as if he didn't hear, and then Mike said, "And Tom here can play all of your tunes." Godfrey looked at me again, this time with a new expression on his face. Like he was looking through a microscope and I was on a slide.

"You a musician?"

"I try to play the trumpet."

Godfrey frowned. "Everybody *tries*. That isn't what I asked you. Are you a *musician*?"

"I'm in a rehearsal band and I'm in my high school orchestra."

"You know something?" Godfrey said to Hitchcock. "Hardly anybody answers questions anymore. Hardly makes talking worthwhile." And he walked away.

Mike and I looked at each other. He was as puzzled as I was. "Mr. Hitchcock," I said, "what answer *should* I have given him?"

The bass player laughed hard, very hard. I didn't think I'd been funny. "Well," he finally said, "I expect he was looking to find out how serious you really are about music, and he couldn't tell from what you said. I couldn't either."

"Serious?" I was shocked. "Why, there's nothing else I'd want to be but a musician. A jazz musician."

"Now we're getting somewhere."

It was then that I got a wild idea in my head. I

4

really didn't know how good I was, if I was any good at all. I mean some of the guys from school I played with called me "young Dizzy" because I had memorized a lot of Dizzy Gillespie solos off his records and I played them without any mistakes. And Mike didn't think I was way out of line when I told him I wanted to forget college and get a job playing. But nobody on the *inside*—no real jazzman—had ever heard me.

"I hope my asking isn't a drag," I said to Hitchcock, "but could I play for you some time? I'd like to get a professional's reaction to my playing."

Hitchcock didn't say anything for a while. He just looked at me with a funny smile. Then he wrote down his address and gave it to me. "Come by Friday afternoon. Around four." I nodded, and he went back inside the Savoy.

I was still full of excitement when I got home and I told my father what had happened. He's a lawyer, but you can talk to him. I mean, Mike's father is a lawyer too, but he comes on at home like he's a high school principal or something. You know, like you have to have an appointment to speak with him. But my father is pretty straight. He doesn't believe I'm as serious about jazz as I am, but he'll learn.

"Where does he live, your bass player friend?"

"In Greenwich Village."

"You ever been in a Negro's home before?" my father asked.

I stopped and thought. You know, I never had. There'd always been some Negro kids in my classes all the way through school, and I'd been pretty friendly with a few of them, but somehow I'd never been in their homes.

"No," I finally said. "Why?"

"I just wanted you to think about it," my father said. He was smiling. "Because I just did. I think your going is a good idea."

That's all he said, and that's why I dig my father. You know, some other father might have made a speech about being careful what I do in a jazz musician's pad. But my father figures I've got some sense. And maybe that's why I do have some—sometimes.

2
The Initiation

I went down to the Village from school on Friday. We live on the East Side in the seventies, in a big apartment building with doormen and elevator operators and all that. But the street on which Hitchcock lived was way west in the Village, near the Hudson River, and it didn't have any apartment houses. And certainly no doormen. There were just a row of old brownstones, a warehouse, a grocery store and a bar. Hitchcock's place was next to the warehouse. I walked up three flights and knocked. A girl answered. Well, a woman, but she was so slim and looked so young that it was hard to believe her when she said, "I'm Mary, Bill's wife. Come in." She couldn't have been more than seventeen, maybe eighteen. The first thing that hit me was how she wore her hair. It was like in pictures I'd seen of African women. Natural. I mean natural for her. It didn't look as if she'd ever been to a beauty parlor. I liked it.

But she sure didn't like me. That was the second thing that hit me. She was very cold. Cold like angry. And I couldn't figure out why. She'd never even seen me before.

"Your white apprentice is here," she called out,

and Hitchcock came out of the kitchen. He wasn't all that friendly either, but at least he didn't seem mad at me. Mostly, I guess, he seemed curious.

"Take out your horn," he said, and he went to the piano at the end of the living room and began to fool around with some chords.

"I didn't know you played piano too," I said.

"It helps me on the bass. There are things about chords you can only really figure out on the piano. Let's play some blues."

He went into a slow blues. I started nervous, but after a while I got into what I felt was a good groove. I didn't make any mistakes, and considering there was no bass or drums, I got a fair pulse going.

"Your friend said you know some of Moses' tunes," Hitchcock said after we'd finished. "How about 'Kenyatta'?"

That was a tricky one. It was hard to improvise on because the chords never went where you expected them to, but I had it down pretty well, and I made it O.K. I mean nobody would have paid to have a record of it but it wasn't a disaster.

We played a few more tunes, and then Hitchcock got up from the piano, filled a pipe, lit it, sat down in an old, dumpy armchair, and looked at me for a long time. I couldn't tell what he was thinking because his face was like a mask. Nothing moved, not even his eyes. I almost shivered, and it was a hot day.

I couldn't stand it anymore, and said, "Well, what did you think?"

"How should I put it?" he said loudly, going over my head to his wife, who was sitting across the room on a stool.

"Tell him like it is," she said, and she smiled at me like I was a fat mouse and she was a cat who had me cornered.

"You've got a good ear," Hitchcock began. "You made some mistakes on the chord changes, but they were hip mistakes. I mean you were trying for something different. That's good. A guy who never makes mistakes because he never takes chances will never be any use in jazz. And your technique is O.K.— for the time you've been playing. About four years?"

He'd hit it exactly right. My father had bought me a horn when I was twelve.

"When are you going to get to where it's at?" his wife said impatiently.

"What I don't hear at all," Hitchcock pulled himself out of a slouch and leaned toward me, "is who *you* are. If you are anybody. It's like you're fooling with the horn. You obviously get kicks out of being able to play as well as you do, but you're not telling any story."

My throat got real dry and I had to cough hard

9

before I could say anything. "You mean," I said, "I haven't got any soul?"

"He means," Mary stood up and walked over to me, "you play that thing as if you've never paid any dues. And you haven't."

"Yeah," Hitchcock said softly, "your blues is like a new pair of shoes. All glossy but no dirt on them because they haven't been anywhere. You know, a lot of guys have written books trying to tell what jazz is, but Charlie Parker told the whole story in less than thirty seconds. He said, 'Music is your own experience, your thoughts, your wisdom. If you don't live it, it won't come out of your horn.' He was talking about all kinds of music, but what he said applies most of all to jazz because when you're improvising, man, you're going inside your*self* to dig out how *you* feel at that moment, and if you haven't lived enough to feel enough, you're not telling any kind of a story that's worth hearing."

I couldn't just sit there and take it all without making some kind of defense. "I'm only sixteen," I said.

"That's not what I'm talking about." Hitchcock looked at his wife. "I've known twelve-year-olds who could hardly blow a scale right but who already were **able** to *make* you hear them talking through their horns."

"Those were *black* twelve-year-olds," his wife said.

Hitchcock didn't go on. "You mean," I said, "I can't play jazz so that it means anything because I'm white?"

"No, I don't mean that," said Hitchcock.

"I do." Mary snapped the words at me like they were a whip, and sure enough, I cringed.

Hitchcock suddenly scowled and got up. "Teaching life ain't my scene," he said. "All I can tell you is you're very young. And I'm not talking about years. Your life has been too easy for you to be making it as a jazz musician."

"And too white," Mary muttered.

"Miss Mau Mau." Hitchcock grinned at her.

There didn't seem to be anything else to say. At least *I* didn't have anything else to say. I got up. "Well, thanks." I started toward the door.

"Don't mention it," said Hitchcock.

I said good-bye to his wife. She just nodded.

"I'd like to come back sometime," I said to Hitchcock.

"You want more punishment?" He laughed. "Yeah, maybe sometime."

So I picked up my horn and left. There was a trash basket in the hallway and I felt for a second like throwing the horn in it. Or myself.

3
Early Blues

For about a week after that afternoon with Hitchcock and his wife, I felt I'd begun to know something about the blues, my own blues. For some guys sports is the big thing. If they make a team or get to be more than just average in some kind of game, they feel they have a corner on being somebody. Like a guy I go to school with. He swims. All year round. And he's some swimmer! He's not much else, but I've noticed that when he gets left out of a conversation, he'll somehow bring the talk around to swimming; and then, for a while, he's in charge. And whenever he's outdone by somebody in something else, he'll mutter, "Well, swimming's *my* thing." Like patting himself on the back. And it works.

For other guys, it's getting good grades or being able to make girls melt. For me, since I was twelve, it's been jazz. I was with my father one Saturday morning and we were walking by a record store in Times Square. I heard somebody playing trumpet, and it was as if that trumpet player were ten feet tall and had just found out that he was going to live forever. I mean, he played as if he were feeling *so* good that he had to let some joy out or he'd explode.

And he made *me* feel glad just to be listening. I had to find out who it was, and so my father and I walked in and we walked out with an LP by Dizzy Gillespie.

From then on all my allowance went on records. More Dizzy and then Miles Davis and Thelonious Monk and Sonny Rollins and Moses Godfrey. When I asked my father for a trumpet, he got one the next day because he'd seen how jazz hit me. The lessons and the practicing were like eating ice cream, because I wanted to get to where I could begin to do what Dizzy and the others did—make the horn talk. Because that's what jazz had always sounded like to me—people talking. Each of them has his own sound, his own way of saying something in the music.

By the time people started asking me what I wanted to be—uncles and grandparents and friends of my father—I'd always answer, "A jazz musician." They'd laugh as if I'd said I wanted to grow up to be a cowboy or a lion tamer, but I was serious. I couldn't have been more serious. And gradually I began to be able to play, to really play that horn. Or so I thought.

A couple of years ago some of the guys where I go to school formed a band for kicks, and I was like its star. We bought stock arrangements and changed them to suit ourselves. Eventually some of us began to write numbers of our own. Everything had been cooking for me until I'd had to ask Bill Hitchcock what he thought of my playing. Now it was as if all those people who'd thought I *had* to be kidding myself about becoming a jazz musician were right. I didn't have it. I wasn't saying anything in my music. And worst of all, I wasn't even the right color.

For once, this wasn't anything I could talk to my father about. He's white too, after all, so I figured he'd have no answer for me either. I did talk to Mike about what had happened.

"It can't be that simple, Tom," Mike said. "Look, what about the white guys who made real contributions to jazz—Bix Beiderbecke, Pee Wee Russell, Stan Getz, Jack Teagarden, Bill Evans? After all, when Miles Davis wanted the best piano player he could get, he hired Bill Evans, didn't he?"

I wanted to believe Mike, but the history of jazz showed something else. Everybody who had made the *big* contributions, who had started a major change that caused everybody to absorb and follow up on what he had discovered—all of those real creators —had been Negro: Louis Armstrong, Duke Ellington, Lester Young, Charlie Parker, Dizzy, Miles, Moses Godfrey. So Mary Hitchcock was right. Who did I think I was, trying to get into that league?

I felt so dragged, I missed a couple of rehearsals

of our band. But not playing made life almost impossible, and I started showing up again. Our band wasn't anything special, but it had always been fun to get together and see what would happen. Now I began to think that the main reason we hadn't been really making it musically was that we had so few Negroes. There were three of them in the band—a good, solid bass player, a pianist who was just beginning to get himself together and had started to make us afraid that he'd soon be too good for us, and an alto saxophonist who had a lot of fire but not much technique.

But three were not enough, and finally I asked Tim, the pianist, if he had any friends who'd like to join the band.

"You mean any colored friends?" He looked at me kind of funny.

"Yes," I said.

"You figure I only have Negro friends, huh?"

It was like being with Mary Hitchcock again. Here I'd asked a simple question and he was treating me like I was a member of the Ku Klux Klan.

I stammered a little and finally said, "No, I meant any of your friends." That wasn't what I'd meant at all, but I figured I was in a corner and that the more I tried to explain myself, the worse things would get.

Tim didn't bring anyone to the next rehearsal,

but Mike had asked the bass player and he did bring a friend. A Negro friend who played trombone. We started out on a simple riff tune that Tim had written, and I was waiting for the new trombonist to solo. He was pretty bad. He didn't swing, his sound was like a frightened horse, and he even lost the beat. Nervousness, I thought, but he didn't get any better all afternoon.

While we were packing up, Tim came over and smiled at me, but it was the kind of smile I'd got from that bartender at the Savoy when I tried to walk inside as if I were entitled to. "All us darkies don't have that thing, do we?" Tim said.

"No," I answered, looking at the trombonist across the room.

"Some of us," said Tim, "are even lousy dancers," and he walked away.

Mike had been listening and he grinned at me. "So where does that leave you now?" Mike asked. "Is skin color still all that important?"

"The fact that one of them can't make it," I said, "doesn't mean that one of us ever really can."

"Boy," said Mike, "you sure make things hard for yourself. Tell me, since all the major classical composers and instrumentalists have been white, does that mean Tim can't make it in *that* league because he's black?"

"It's not the same thing," I said.

"Why not?"

I didn't know why not. I guess I hadn't thought it all the way through. "You want to go stand outside the Savoy tonight?" I asked Mike, avoiding the question.

He dug I didn't want to answer, and we agreed where we'd meet to go downtown.

At dinner that night my father questioned me about how the music was going, and I asked him what would be good to major in if I decided to go to college with the idea of being a lawyer. He looked surprised. "Thought you were going to be a jazz musician."

"No, that's just for kicks. I mean I need a *profession*." I felt like crying when I said it, and then I thought of Mary Hitchcock. O.K., I'm not living in a room with rats and there's no place I can't go if I have the money to pay, but I'm paying *some* kind of dues right now. Then it was as if I could hear her answering, "Poor white boy, those shoes aren't even scuffed yet—and you think you have the blues!"

4
Getting Inside

The intermission trio was on when we got to the Savoy, and out on the sidewalk were Moses Godfrey, Bill Hitchcock, and Bill's wife, Mary. I wanted to nod and just walk right by, but Mike stopped. He started asking Hitchcock about a new record he was on. Godfrey stared out into space, patting his beard gently. Mary took him by the arm. "Want some coffee, Moses?" she asked. He smiled, touched her hand, and stood just where he was, looking straight ahead.

A black Cadillac drove up. The white chauffeur got out and held the back door open. A fat lady inside waved at Godfrey. She looked like she'd dressed in three minutes. I mean she had a fur coat on over a blouse and slacks, and she was wearing sneakers. Godfrey stepped forward with a smile, Mary Hitchcock gave her a big grin and then kissed her on the cheek. I hadn't been able to imagine Mary ever looking glad to see anyone white. Bill Hitchcock nodded at the lady pleasantly, and they all went inside.

"Who was that?" Mike asked, his mouth open.

A very dark Negro, who had been leaning against the window of the Savoy, said, "That lady is the hope of the world." He laughed. "And you *know* there's not much hope for *this* world."

We stayed to hear the music. It was one of the best Moses Godfrey sets I'd ever heard. The thing that makes jazz so exciting is you never know when that time is going to come when *everyone* in a group is on fire. A lot of the time, one or two players are having a fine night but the others are just cooling it. I don't mean they make mistakes, but they're not "cooking." You're cooking when you can play everything that jumps into your mind. Your fingers practically go where they're supposed to before you're even aware what you're going to play next; and when that happens, your horn is a part of you—like your arms or your feet. And when everyone in a jazz combo is at that level, the experience is the most exciting I know.

That's the way Godfrey and Hitchcock and the others were playing that night. At midnight Mike said he had to go home, but I couldn't leave. I couldn't take the chance of missing another set like that. So I stayed on that sidewalk until three in the morning. And when the music had stopped, even then I couldn't leave. I stood rooted there like I had been put into a trance by some magician. Inside my head the music was still playing and I didn't want to jar it loose by walking.

Finally the musicians came out, along with Mary and the fat lady. Moses, Bill Hitchcock and his wife, and the fat lady started to get into the Cadillac. Moses looked at me and said, "You're the one who's *trying* to be a musician?" I nodded. "Come on in." He gestured toward the car. Mary frowned and Bill looked surprised. The other lady smiled at me and said, "I'm Veronica. We're going to my house to listen to records and play some ping-pong. You're welcome."

I hoped my parents were long since asleep. One of them usually waited up for me, and besides, I was never supposed to be home later than eleven unless it was a dance or something like that. But a chance to spend some time with Moses Godfrey made me brave. So I figured my father would understand, and if he did, he could calm my mother down. I got in the car.

It only took about ten minutes to drive to Veronica's house in the Village. She lived in a brownstone on Tenth Street near Washington Square. On the way, nobody spoke at first. Moses was humming a song. I'd never heard it before but I was sure it was something he'd made up. It had those sudden turns that sounded like punch lines at the end of a very funny story.

"Something new, Moses?" Hitchcock asked.

"Old, man," said Godfrey. "I've been working on this one for almost a year. It takes a l-o-o-o-o-n-g time to write something. Everything has to fit just right. The middle has to go with the ends; the ends have to go with each other. It has to sound as if it always was, as if nobody made it up, as if it were just waiting for somebody to come along and find it and play it."

"What's it called?" Veronica asked.

"It's called 'Veronica's Waiting.'"

Veronica was so pleased she smiled all the way to her house. We went up a flight of stairs and through a red door. To the right of the door was a big living room with a long couch, a lot of deep, soft chairs, an enormous hi-fi set, and more records than I'd ever seen outside of a store. There were records all over the place—on the couch, on the chairs, and on a small table next to the hi-fi set. She seemed to have everything that anybody important in jazz had made. As I looked through the piles, what hit me was she didn't have anything even remotely square. She seemed to be at least fifty, and yet she was hipper than the kids I knew who *thought* they were so hip.

Godfrey sat down, got up again, motioned to Hitchcock, and they went into the next room. There was a ping-pong table, and they went at it. They were laughing but they were playing like demons. They fought out each point as if the loser was going to have his head cut off. Bill being so lean and quick and with a much longer reach, I thought he'd win easily. But Godfrey got his short, stocky frame around as if he were on wheels, and he beat Bill twenty-one to ten.

They started another game and I went back into the living room. Veronica and Mary were listening to one of Moses' records, and across the room a young, slender blonde girl about my age was reading a book. She looked up. "I'm Jessica, Veronica's daughter."

I told her who I was and asked her, "Does Godfrey come here often?"

"He practically lives here," she said. "On the second floor there's a room with a grand piano that's his any time he wants it. When he's working on new music he often stays in there for days. Except to eat, of course. He has his own place, but he seems to like it here better."

"I'm surprised your mother is so hip about jazz. I mean, it's unusual a woman her age—"

Jessica laughed. "She picked up on jazz when she was just a kid. Her older brother was a record collector and she just stayed with it."

"Does your father dig the music too?"

Jessica paused for a moment. "He's dead," she said. "Last year. No, he didn't get much out of jazz. But he liked Mother so much that he was always trying to get with the music."

It was so easy talking to Jessica. She wasn't like most of the girls I knew. You asked her a question and she answered. Straight. No fencing or teasing.

"We've had jazz in the house," she went on, "as far back as I can remember. Instead of children's records before bedtime, mother would play Louis Armstrong and Pee Wee Russell and Fats Waller. They were so funny. I mean they made me laugh."

"Have you always lived in New York?"

"Oh, no. Before my father died, we traveled a lot. He was in the State Department and we lived in quite a few countries." Jessica leaned forward, grinning. "And everywhere we went, cases of records went too. You see, Daddy found out jazz worked for *him*. He made a lot of contacts faster through jazz than he might have otherwise."

"I don't dig."

"You can't imagine," Jessica said, "how many young editors and labor union people, and even a few cabinet ministers here and there, sat on the floor in our living room asking for another side by Miles or Dizzy or Duke. Daddy even began reading *Down Beat* so he could make some intelligent conversation with them about jazz."

Veronica had put another record on the machine. It was by a new tenor player who was supposed to be very radical. One of the critics had said that all of the jazz to come would go the way this new guy was going. I'd found it hard to follow what he was doing most of the time. He got some very strange sounds out of his horn, and his tunes sounded as if they were made up of bits and pieces that didn't really fit into anything you could remember as a whole piece.

Godfrey came back into the room and listened. He went over to the machine and played the same track over three times.

"What do you think?" Veronica asked.

"I'm not thinking," said Moses. "I'm feeling. I'll think about what he does later if I'm interested. Right now I want to hear his story."

"What kind of story do you hear?" Mary looked at him, clearly curious to hear what he had to say.

"I hear"—Godfrey plopped down on the sofa— "a young man, a very young man, who has had a lot of trouble getting people to listen to him, to see him, to know that he even exists."

I didn't say anything, but I was puzzled. How could Godfrey figure that out from just a few bars of music? We listened to two more numbers by the tenor.

"Anything else?" Mary asked Godfrey.

"He's got a lot of things he's trying to tear out of himself." Godfrey said. "Ugly things." Godfrey caught the question on my face and laughed. "You think I'm coming on like some gypsy fortune-teller?"

24

"No," I said, startled and kind of embarrassed. "It's just that I don't know how you get all that out of a few solos."

"It's no mystery, boy." Godfrey leaned back and stretched. "If you listen long enough, you find out a lot more about musicians from what they play than from what they say. Now this cat"—he gestured toward the record player—"isn't all that clear himself yet about what he's saying. He's just beginning to get himself together with that horn."

"He's no amateur, Moses," said Mary.

"Oh." Moses was exasperated. "I'm not talking about what he can do *technically*. I mean he's going through that time when he has to shoot out everything he feels and thinks. Like every solo is the last one he's going to play. Later, he'll start thinking about what to leave *out* as well as what to put in."

"Take the record with you, Moses." Veronica moved toward the record player.

"No," said Godfrey. "First I want to hear him in a club for a while. Get to know him firsthand. Records are like a picture album. Good to have around when you want to go back in time. But they can't surprise you. And I like to be surprised."

Godfrey leaned back and closed his eyes, and in a few seconds he was asleep. I must have looked as surprised as I felt, because Jessica said, "Moses does what he feels like. Always. He felt sleepy, so he went

25

to sleep. If he's hungry, he'll eat eight times in one day. And the next day he might not eat at all."

The music and conversation continued as though Godfrey weren't there. Bill Hitchcock sat down beside me and asked how my music was going. "O.K.," I said. And then I couldn't resist adding, "Considering my color."

"We really shook you up the other day?"

"Not you so much," I told him, "but your wife. She left me with no place to go but out of jazz. I can't change my skin."

Hitchcock lit his pipe. "Why have you got such a thing about jazz? Why not girls or spaceships?"

I didn't answer right away. I dig a lot of sports and I like girls, although I can't stay long with a girl who doesn't like jazz too. I guess the thing is that everything I do like leads one way or another to jazz. "Because," I finally said, "I never feel better than when I'm playing. Everything comes together then. I mean, when I'm playing, it's like everything I dig and everything I don't dig come out in the music. Am I making any sense?"

"Yeah," said Hitchcock. "I know what you're talking about. Maybe you do have something to say on that horn."

"I'm not trying to cop out, but I was playing it too safe that afternoon at your house. I didn't want to make any mistakes. So I was playing the notes, you know, but not much else."

"Could be," Hitchcock nodded. "You want to come back?"

"Sure," I said and then looked across the room at Mary. "But—but how about your wife?"

Hitchcock laughed. "Yes?"

"She makes me feel way on the outside."

"It's about time"—Hitchcock leaned back—"you started knowing the Marys among us. If you want to be any part of the jazz scene, you're going to have to be able to feel a draft sometimes without catching cold. Besides, she's not as ferocious as she might have seemed. She digs Veronica, after all."

I looked across the room. Mary and Veronica were giggling at a story that Veronica was telling. "How did Veronica break through?" I asked. "I mean, is she with CORE or one of the other civil rights groups or something?"

Hitchcock looked at me as if I was from Mars. "Boy, you have a lot to learn. She 'broke through,' as you put it, very simply. By being herself. It may take time, but that's the only way to make it. In anything that counts."

"Ah"—Godfrey was awake—"I hear the sound of a tailor weaving the emperor's clothes. Generalities. Generalities."

"Where did I goof, Moses?" Hitchcock seemed annoyed.

"You tell that boy to be himself. What self? If he's like most people, he's one boy at school. He's another boy in the street. He's a third boy with his father. And a fourth boy with his mother. And umpteen different kinds of boys at other times and places."

"Oh, man," said Hitchcock, "you know what I'm talking about. There comes a time, or there should, when all those different selves get linked up, and no matter what you're doing, you're basically one kind of person. That's when you can start cooking —when you've sorted out all those different selves, thrown away the ones that are phony and worked on getting the others into some kind of a whole."

"At sixteen?" said Godfrey.

"How did you know how old I was?" I asked.

"When I was sixteen," said Godfrey, "I worked at a carnival. I guessed people's ages and I guessed their weight. I also guessed how alive they were, but I didn't tell them *that*."

"Would you tell me?" I was afraid he would.

"I will tell you a story," said Godfrey.

Veronica shut off the hi-fi machine. She, Mary, and Jessica came over and sat on the floor. Hitchcock leaned back in his chair, puffing his pipe. For some reason I felt very young. It was almost like waiting in the nursery for my father to tell me a story before I went to bed. And that was long, long ago. Ten years. But the story Moses Godfrey told wasn't anything like the ones my father made up. I can still hear Godfrey's high, soft voice. Sometimes it got so soft I could hardly make out what he was saying, and underneath the story it was as if a song was being played. In the silences between the words I could almost actually hear it. But mostly, I just felt it. I know it sounds crazy to talk about feeling music when there is no music being played. But it can happen. And what I felt was a blues, an old, old blues that came out of a time and a place I knew nothing about. But somehow it was familiar. As familiar as breathing. Anyway, this is the story he told. He took off his dark glasses to tell it.

5
"Big Charlie"

Like I said, when I was your age, I was working in a traveling carnival. I'd been born in Harlem, never knew my father, and when my mother died, soon after I was two, I'd been given to my mother's sister. "Given" isn't quite the word. She was my mother's only living relative, and although I'm sure she would rather have put me out for adoption—or better yet, just lost me somewhere—her religion made her take me in. She had an image of herself as a good, God-fearing woman; and a good, God-fearing woman took care of small relatives with no place else to go.

My aunt, Alberta, worked as a maid, cook, baby nurse, heavy cleaner, and laundress for a white lady downtown. She left at seven in the morning and came back at eight at night. She got thirty dollars a week, leftover food, high blood pressure, and a bad disposition. She was so tired when she got home she had no patience to listen to a child. She had so much to do on Sunday—her one day off—she had no time for me then either. She had to go to church, clean her own house, and go to church again. So I grew up in a silent house. Only times she ever said anything to me was to tell me to do something. Or more often, not to do something.

I spent all the time I could in the street when I wasn't in school because there was noise and life out on that street. I also went into the cellar a lot, because the super in our building had a section down there for himself and in it he kept an old, beat-up piano somebody had thrown out years ago. The keys stuck, the sound was like hitting a cracked dish with a fork, and the pedal was long since gone. But I made it play. Mostly I played what I heard in my head, and later the super—who had been a musician when he was young—taught me a little about chords. The little he knew.

By the time I was ten, I'd started sneaking out at night when my aunt fell asleep. I hung around outside bars with music in them, listening especially to the piano players and then trying the next day to play what I'd heard the night before. After a while, I also played piano in my aunt's church. It was one of those storefront churches, and practically the whole service was music—shouting, stomping, singing with me underneath. They didn't pay me anything, but the piano was better than the super's in the cellar and I enjoyed hearing the notes sound like they were supposed to. Besides, I liked that church music. Once you got in that groove, you could really lose yourself. You became part of the shouting and the pounding. You forgot how old and dirty your neighborhood was. You forgot you were in a black ghetto. Until the music stopped and you were outside again.

I left school when I was fifteen. It was either me or it. The teachers treated us like we were in a zoo and they were the keepers. Since they came on that way, some of us acted like we were in a cage trying to break down the bars. That made the teachers worse, so there were no kicks in going to school. Nobody talked to us about going to college. The most they said was that we had to learn some kind of trade, like being a mechanic or an electrician. But I hardly saw any black mechanics or electricians when I was growing up, so I figured they were conning us. Besides, my trade was going to be music and they sure didn't teach us anything about jazz in school.

Leaving meant leaving my aunt. To her it was very simple. If you cut out of school, you were no good and you were bound to get worse. She kept jawing at me to go back, and her putting me down all the time was worse than the silence. So I went to the super and I asked him if he'd lend me bus fare somewhere.

He did and he gave me the address of a man he'd

known many years ago in Kansas City when he'd
been a musician. That man was still there and he
got me the job in the carnival. It was a show that
traveled through the Southwest, playing sometimes
in open lots and sometimes in theatres in Negro
neighborhoods. My main job was playing for the
dancers and the singers, but to make extra money,
I also guessed people's ages and weights before and
after each performance.

I had a good time. In each town, I had a chance
to hear all the local musicians, and a few even gave
me some lessons whenever I passed through. And
in one town, Dallas, I met Big Charlie Wilkins. He
was a big, blind old man who played guitar and
sang in the streets. It seemed like he knew all the
blues that had ever been made up and he kept adding some new ones of his own. His voice was thick
and raw, and he grunted as much as he sang and
sometimes he'd just holler. All of a sudden he'd give
a big whoop, bang hard on the guitar, and shout, "I
feel like hollering because this town is so small!"
And everybody would get out of his way.

Other times he'd sing slow and sad and he could
make you cry. He'd sing about being hungry or
lonely or both. Once in a while he'd even sing funny
songs—about animals that were smarter than people
and about big bullies that got good and tricked

33

by little black men. He made enough money on the street to eat and to pay a few dollars rent every month on an old shack in the backyard of a friend of his. Big Charlie had never married, but a lot of the kids in the colored section would follow him around and he'd tell them stories or make up songs for them when he was in a good mood. So you could say he had a lot of children without having to worry about feeding them and keeping them in school. To me at that time, he seemed at least a hundred years old, but he was just half that. And he had a long way to go.

First time I was in Dallas I saw Big Charlie, and I followed him around listening to him sing. After a few blocks he turned and said, "You think that's right, taking in all that music for free and not giving nothing back?" I gave him half a dollar and walked beside him. That afternoon when he was through, he said I could come with him to his shack. I had a couple of hours until our show began, and I went along.

From the outside the shack looked like a good holler would blow it away. There were no windows, and it leaned a little like somebody had already started to push it down. Inside it was something else! On the floor was one of the biggest and most

beautiful rugs I'd ever seen. It was purple and yellow
with all kinds of complicated designs woven all the
way through it.

"Feels good, huh?" Big Charlie said when we
came in.

It felt like walking in a big movie house I'd once
been in. It felt like walking in a palace, I guess. At
least the way I imagined a palace might be. There
were a couple of big armchairs, a large mahogany
table that was so polished you could begin to see
yourself in it, a kerosene lamp, and—also on the
rug—a potbellied stove. And everything was so
clean even my aunt would have been satisfied.

"Ain't no reason an old, blind black man can't
have comfort, is there?" said Big Charlie.

"No," I answered.

"Ain't no reason he can't be free either," Charlie
went on, settling down in one of the chairs and sigh-
ing contentedly.

"Free?" I asked. "Free and black in Texas?"

"You was with me all day," Charlie said. "Didn't
see me do anything I didn't want to, did you? Didn't
see me shining anyone's shoes or saying, 'Yassuh,
boss.' I was just singing for my friends and if they
had money to give me because they liked it, I took it.
Mind you, I'm not saying it's easy to be free down

here. To be safe, I got to stay out of the white folk's neighborhood, but I got it worked out so that within my own territory I'm my own man.

"Only way I can do that," Big Charlie went on, "is because I can sing and play. If I didn't have that, I'd have to crawl and I'd have to grin when I didn't see nothing funny."

"But why do you stay in Dallas at all?" I asked. "You'd be even freer up North?"

"Would I? Where you come from?"

"Harlem."

"You free up there?"

I didn't answer because he knew the answer.

"Someday," said Big Charlie, "we going to get really free everywhere, North and South, but in the meantime, I take care of myself and I do a pretty good job. Look at this." He put his hand underneath the mahogany table, and I heard something click. There was a panel and from inside the opening, Charlie took out a long, square box covered in blue velvet.

He put the box on the table and opened it. Inside was a silver flute, the biggest gold watch I'd ever seen, and a book bound in red leather.

"Now, I don't know you, boy, and I suppose you could just pick up these things and run." Charlie laughed. "But the only way I been able to last is to have faith in my feelings. And I feel you're straight. Now, I play that flute when I'm all by myself. That's no horn to bring out into the street, but by myself I make up stories and pictures whichever way the melodies go on that flute. It's my own movies. And that watch was my daddy's. He was a piano player and he gambled some and he liked good times. He was a free man too—until he stepped over the line."

"What line?"

"The line of his territory. He was in a strange town in Georgia, playing in a cafe, and when he finished his job one night, he saw some white men beating up on a colored boy. He made a mistake. He tried to help him."

"And?"

"After they got through with him, his hands couldn't even hold on to a glass of water. Ever."

I could tell Charlie didn't want to talk about his father anymore and I asked him about the book. He brightened. "A man give me that one day. He knew I was blind, but he said the book might make me feel good sometimes. And it has. People sometimes read to me from it."

I expected it was a Bible, but when I opened it, the title page read:

Music

AND SOME HIGHLY MUSICAL

PEOPLE

CONTAINING
BRIEF CHAPTERS ON

I. A Description of Music.

II. The Music of Nature.

III. A Glance at the History of Music.

IV. The Power, Beauty and Uses of Music.

Following Which Are Given Sketches of the Lives
of Remarkable Musicians of the Colored Race

With Portraits

And an Appendix Containing Copies of Music

COMPOSED BY COLORED MEN

The author was James M. Trotter and the book had been published in Boston in 1880.

"There's a marker in there," said Big Charlie. "Read to me from where the marker is."

On the page in which the marker had been set, a big black arrow pointed to a paragraph. Later I copied it out and memorized it along with the title page.

Yesterday evening I walked, late in the moonlight, in the beautiful avenue of lime trees on the bank of the Rhine; and I heard a tapping noise and soft singing. At the door of a cottage, under the blooming lime tree, sat a mother and her twin-babies: the one lay at her breast, the other in a cradle, which she rocked with her foot, keeping time to her singing. In the very germ, then, when the first trace of life begins to stir, music is the nurse of the soul: it murmurs in the ear, and the child sleeps; the tones are companions of his dreams; they are the world in which he lives. He has nothing; the babe, although cradled in his mother's arms, is alone in the spirit; but tones find entrance into the self-conscious soul, and nourish it as earth nourishes the life of plants.

Charlie had me read it again, smiling all the while. "Now," he said, "except for my guitar and this place and the things in that box, I ain't got much more than I had when I came into this world. But I've always had music, and that's what keeps me going. A man's lucky when he's able to keep growing his own food, no matter what else happens. And music is my food."

The next time I saw Big Charlie—about six months later—we spent another late afternoon in his shack. He played his flute and it was like there were two Charlies. On the street, his singing and playing was rugged and full of hot, harsh colors— even when it was soft. But when he played the flute, the music was cool and flowing. He could play the blues on the flute too, but it was like blues from another world, a world where nobody ever got hurt or died. And that blues was like a song of sorrow that everybody couldn't live in that other world.

"And now I'm going to teach you something," Big Charlie said. "Come back when your show is through."

It was after midnight when I came back to the shack. Big Charlie got up and we walked a few blocks until we came to a street of bars, poolrooms, cafes, and a dancehall. "I want you to watch and listen," said Big Charlie, "and try to remember everything."

For the next two hours, Big Charlie would hear a voice and then point out men and women who hardly ever saw the day. One way or another, they all made their living·on that street. Some seemed to be unable to say anything without yelling. Others hardly said anything at all and had the look of some- one who'd just stolen something. Still others seemed always ready for a fight—even if they had to make one up. Charlie talked to all of them, drew them out, asked them how they were doing, what was bugging them. Since I was with him, they didn't give me any trouble although most of them looked at me curiously.

On the way back to the shack Charlie asked me to describe the people I'd met. I managed to remember most of them. "Now tell me what you think each of them is like," Charlie said. I did, and when I was through, he shook his head. "Wrong. Most of the time wrong. The man you said was probably a murderer is one of the most sweet men in this whole city. Down at bottom. Sure, he hollers and roars, but that shows how much life he has in him. If he feels rotten inside, he gets it out of him fast, so nothing backs up in him. And the most dangerous man you met all night was that whisper- ing man with the big words. Didn't you hear how flat he spoke, how careful he spoke? That man's had most of his life battered out of him by trying to crash through those big white walls that keep him

41

here. He's got no faith left in himself and in no one else either. And not feeling good about himself, he ain't about to do anybody any good.

"You're a musician," Charlie said. "And a musician has to listen so that you'll keep learning more things to say in your music, and you got to listen to protect yourself. A traveling musician's going to be alone in strange towns most of the time, and you got to know who to trust and who not to trust. And you trust those people with the most life in them. You can tell by listening *underneath* what they say. By the pitch of their voices, by how they laugh, by how they listen to you and what they ask you. There's a lot of ways. The main thing is to always *listen*. Being blind, I got nothing else to do *but* listen. And I know more about most people I meet a few times than they know about themselves. I know a lot about you. Like you didn't have no mother or father."

I hadn't told him much about myself and I certainly hadn't told him I'd been raised by an aunt.

"And," said Charlie, "you been hearing different music in your head than what you're playing. It's so different, you're afraid to let it out because people will laugh at you. Let it out, boy, let it out. If you don't, it'll give you no peace."

And that's how my "style," as the critics put it,

began. I finally did begin to play what I heard. It got me fired from the carnival because the boss called it "Chinese music." And it got me fired from a lot of jobs, until finally other musicians began to pick up on what I was doing and I didn't sound so unusual anymore. Then I heard other new things and began to play *them,* but by that point I'd proved myself so nobody laughed anymore.

Last time I saw Big Charlie was three years ago. He'd heard I'd been making it and he was very pleased. I told him how much he'd helped, but he said the music would have come out anyway. He'd heard a record of mine and he said my music was too strong to be bottled up too long. When we said good-bye, he gave me his watch. I didn't really look at it until I got to the hotel room that night, and I was amazed that it still kept time. Nearly perfect time. Big Charlie had wound that watch every day.

6
No Heroes in the Park

Godfrey finished his story, took out the gold watch, rubbed it fondly, opened the case, checked the time against the wristwatch on his right hand, and smiled. "It's still cooking," he said.

"Could you tell me how alive I am?" I asked him.

"Not now," said Godfrey. "Another time, another place."

It was getting light, and I suddenly came back to my own world and wondered whether my parents had realized I hadn't come home. I got up, said goodbye, ran outside, and took a cab home.

Mostly I was worried about what my father would say. I don't mean I don't dig my mother. It's just that these last few years, we don't have very much to say to each other. She's always after me to eat right and wear my rubbers and do my homework, but there isn't much I can talk to her about when it comes to things that really matter to me. Like when I come in with a new record, she still says, "Another one? I don't know why you keep buying them. They all sound alike." She's not being mean, but she just doesn't understand. My father, he doesn't talk nearly so much as she does, but when I come to him with something that's bothering me, he usually gets right down to where it is.

There was a light on in the living room, and there was my father, asleep over a book. I stumbled against a lamp and he shook awake. I told him what had happened and how important it had been for me to spend some time with Godfrey.

"I should be angrier than I am," he said, "but I *am* disappointed. You usually care about other people's feelings, and for all we knew, you might have been in an accident. You could have phoned, you know."

I admitted he was right and he dropped the subject. That's what I mean about him. Once he makes a point, he doesn't keep drilling it into you. We talked about the story of Big Charlie for a while and then I told him I was undecided again about college.

"What if I did decide," I asked, "to go into jazz full-time after high school? Would you be terribly upset?"

My father lit a cigarette and blew smoke for a few seconds. "I wouldn't be delighted, but I'm not about to force you to go to college. I think, though, you'd be making a mistake. Freedom is a big thing in jazz, isn't it?"

"Sure, that's what it's all about."

"Well, are you freer knowing just a few chords or knowing a whole lot of chords?"

"I get your point," I said, "but what I'm not sure of is whether college is the place to learn the kinds of things *I* want to know. And not only about music."

He sort of half smiled, said we'd talk about it some more, and we both went to bed.

The next day in school I told Mike about the night with Godfrey and my talk with my father.

"I don't know about the college scene," said Mike, "George Bernard Shaw said that if he was educating a kid, he'd just give him a list of the right books to read. And you could do that kind of studying days and play at night. But I still think you're exaggerating this color thing. What about Django Reinhardt? A lot of Negro jazzmen, and not only guitarists, had a lot of respect for him."

"But he was a gypsy."

"Good lord." Mike shook his head. "You keep inventing new ways to make yourself an alien."

"But I am an alien," I said. "I'm white and I'm Anglo-Saxon way back and my parents are Protestants. I'm a WASP, Mike. Ain't many of us in the jazz history books."

"You're impossible and I'm late for class. Maybe you could do what that writer John Howard Griffin did. Get yourself dyed deep brown."

I felt a great need to talk to Moses Godfrey again, and that night, after telling my father I'd be back early, I went down to the Savoy.

Godfrey wasn't there. Hitchcock told me he hadn't shown up, hadn't called, and no one knew where he was.

"Did you call his home?" I asked.

"Nobody," said Hitchcock. "can reach Moses at his home. He has no phone, and you can't go see him unless he asks you. No matter what. If you do, that's the end of any relationship you have with Moses."

I left, and began to walk toward Greenwich Village. All the way, I was juggling in my mind whether I ought to go to college or try to make the jazz scene. I walked toward Washington Square Park. It was about ten when I got there and the park was nearly deserted. A couple of men were sitting, staring into space. A few couples walked along, holding hands. And sitting on the rim of the fountain was a short, bulky figure I thought I recognized. It was Godfrey. He was patting the gold watch and looking up into the sky.

I walked over and said quickly, "If I'm disturbing you, I'll walk on."

He didn't seem surprised to see me. "Sit down," he said.

"You been by the Savoy?" he asked.

"They're wondering where you are."

"They'll wonder a while longer. I'll make it. And I'll play the rest of the night without intermission. That'll even it up."

I noticed a group of boys watching us. There were about ten of them and they looked to be about my age or a little older.

"Who's your black friend?" one of them yelled.

"Maybe they're both black—inside," another said as they came closer. He was laughing and it was the kind of laugh my math teacher uses when he's about to tell us most of us flunked.

"Pay them no mind," said Godfrey. He'd become the way he was when I first saw him outside the Savoy—distant, not part of the scene.

They were in front of us.

"You suppose that's a real beard, Chino?"

Suddenly one of them—it must have been Chino—reached out, grabbed Godfrey's beard, and pulled hard. With his other hand, he snatched off Godfrey's dark glasses. There was no reaction from Godfrey. He stared straight ahead. I thought I'd run and get a cop, but it was too late. We were now in the middle of a circle.

"Do you suppose *he's* real, Chino—the black rabbi's friend?"

A punch in my stomach knocked all the wind out of me.

"Hey," one of them yelled, "wait a minute. That's Moses Godfrey!"

"So?" said Chino, starting toward us again. I had two choices. I could start swinging and have all of them pile on me or I could try to protect my mouth. A couple of good punches there and I wouldn't be able to play for weeks. Before I could do either, the boy who had recognized Godfrey pulled Chino back.

"He's a musician, man," the boy said. "Let him alone."

"He's black," said Chino.

"Let him alone!" The boy had a knife in his hand and moved toward Chino.

Chino backed away from him—and from us. "O.K., O.K.," he muttered. "If it's all that important." Chino, scowling, walked off. The others followed him.

"Ain't that something?" Godfrey seemed to be talking more to himself than to me. "A hood saves me from other hoods because somehow the music got to him. But that's so little. That saved only me this time. If I'd been some other black cat, I'd be on the ground with maybe my head bashed in. Ain't that something?"

Godfrey was silent for a minute and then he started again. "If that was Big Charlie, he'd have been on the ground because he hasn't been in any maga-

49

zines or made any records. Free! Free? Ain't that something?" Godfrey was crying. I was embarrassed and looked down at my shoes.

"Boy"—he turned to me—"go away."

I went. I felt terrible. First of all, seeing all that hate, that crazy hate on Chino's face, had made me sick. I mean really sick. And I felt worse when I remembered I'd only been thinking about saving myself. I hadn't thought of Godfrey at all when we were caught in that circle.

I decided to take a chance that Jessica was home and would talk to me. She'd been easy to talk to that night, and right now I couldn't stand being alone.

Veronica opened the door. Jessica, she told me, was out. "But come in, Tom," she said. I followed her into that huge living room. She gave me a Coke and put on a new album by Dizzy Gillespie. Hearing Dizzy was like getting a transfusion.

While the album was still playing, the doorbell rang and Mary Hitchcock came in. She gave me a cold eye, sat down on the other side of the room, and began to read *Down Beat*. The record ended, and I told Veronica what had happened. "For no reason," I said. "For no reason they were going to clobber us. And then one of them recognized Moses. A hood who digs jazz. Isn't that something? And he made them lay off."

"And what were *you* doing?" Mary asked. Her eyes were blazing.

"I didn't do anything. I didn't try to help Moses. I just wanted to get out of there. I was thinking I'd run and get a cop, but I guess the truth is I just wanted to run."

I sat there, waiting for the whip, and I got it.

"Some hero!" Mary looked at me as if I ought to be squashed.

"But what else could he have done?" said Veronica.

"He could have put himself between them and Moses, that's what he could have done. That man Moses is important."

"Would *you* have?" Veronica turned to her.

"Of course," said Mary. "Moses is much more valuable than I am."

"Would you, if it was a valuable *white* man who was being threatened?" Veronica wasn't asking like a district attorney. Her voice was very gentle.

"Ain't no valuable white man," Mary said stiffly.

"Well, now"—I heard a soft, high voice—"what if he were only half white, or quarter white, or one-eighth white? How would you *know*, Mary? How would you know in time?" It was Godfrey. I hadn't been aware of his having come in. Maybe the door had been left open. Maybe he had a key.

"Look at me," said Godfrey. "I had a white grandmother and my father was at least half Indian. How much of *me* would you protect?"

Mary grinned. "All right, all right. You been appointed Brotherhood Negro of the week?"

"That's not my point," said Godfrey. "You're the one who's making up rules. As for me, if ten guys were surrounding me and somebody else—even if that somebody else were Thelonious Monk or Martin Luther King—I don't know that I'd be thinking about protecting anybody but me. Oh, if one of my kids was with me, it would be different. Or," he added, "Big Charlie."

It was the first time I knew Godfrey had children. None of the magazines had said anything about his even being married. But this clearly wasn't the time to ask him about them. He was in an odd mood. Not angry and not detached but full of impatience. He went to a telephone next to the hi-fi machine and called the Savoy. "I won't be in tonight," he said into the phone. "You tell the people I'm sick. Sick of being comfortable." He hung up. "Tell Bill," he said to Mary, "we got a rehearsal tomorrow. Three o'clock. My house. Tell him to call the others." He started to leave and then looked at me. "You want to learn something, boy, you come too. Mary will tell you where it is." And Godfrey left.

Mary was reluctant to give me the address, but did.

"I don't know what he thinks he's going to find in you, boy," she said, as she handed me a slip of paper. "You've got nothing for him."

"Maybe Moses likes to give sometimes," Veronica said.

"Then he ought to give to his own," Mary answered, and on that happy note, she left.

Left alone with Veronica, I suddenly felt very envious of her. She was on the inside. She didn't seem conscious of any color barrier when she talked with Mary or Godfrey or any of the other Negroes who fell into her place like it was partly theirs.

"How did you get inside?" I finally blurted out.

She looked at me and laughed. Not *at* me. More like laughing to herself. She got up and started moving around the room as she talked. For a big woman, she moved very gracefully. I mean she like flowed.

"Inside?" she started. "Why am I accepted, you mean? Well, I'm not entirely. No one ever can be. There are some Negro musicians who refuse to come here. They think I think I'm slumming when I hang out with jazzmen. And I've never tried to persuade them otherwise, because you can't. If they ever do come by and relax, then they'll make up their minds on the basis of what they know, not what they imagine. Besides, some of them I wouldn't want to be friendly with anyway—whether they were

53

green or purple or pink. The main thing, though, is you can't *force* anybody to see you as you want to be seen. You just do what you do. And some people you dig will dig you. And some won't."

"You mean I've been pressing too hard?"

"In a way, I suppose. But that's natural since this is all so new to you and you so desperately want to be let in."

"But how did it start with you?" I asked. "Jessica told me your brother collected records and you picked up on jazz from him. But what about knowing the musicians?"

"My brother," Veronica answered, "was the only person I could talk to at home. My father was a doctor. He was away lots of the time and my mother was very, very social. I saw much more of my nurse than I ever did of her. Then, when my brother left home, I was really alone. And I kept being alone all through school. Practically everybody I knew seemed so controlled, so disciplined. Sometimes I'd want to shout or cry or just do a somersault out of feeling good; but if I had, everyone else I knew would have thought me a kook."

"And your husband?"

"A nice man, a gentle man. But I never was able to talk much with him either. Let alone shout or do somersaults. But as I grew older, my brother introduced me to a few musicians. He's a physicist, but he still collects records, plays pretty good piano, and makes the clubs. Through him I met some people—a trumpet player in Ellington's band, Moses, a bass player with Basie—with whom I gradually became very friendly. I guess it happened because I really wasn't asking anything of them. I wasn't a band chick or a fan in the may-I-have-your-autograph sense. We simply had some common interests. Not only jazz. The trumpet player knows a great deal about the French Impressionist painters, and so do I. And Moses knows so much about Negro history, a field I've been reading in since I was a girl. The bass player is a fine cook, and we spend hours remembering menus."

Veronica sat down again, leaned back, and continued: "Through them, I met other jazzmen with whom I had other interests in common. And the ones I liked best were people who were very spontaneous. They told you exactly what they thought and exactly how they felt. It wasn't that they weren't disciplined when they had to be, but they didn't hold themselves in all the time. And since *they* were free, I was able to become freer."

"You kind of forgot they were Negro and they forgot you were white?"

"In a way. You know, Negroes aren't acutely

conscious of being black twenty-four hours a day every day. They were themselves and I was myself. So, young man, that's how I got 'inside,' as you put it. With some jazz musicians. Not many. You never do get inside with very many people. Of any color."

"But it does take a lot of time?" I asked rather anxiously.

"The more you worry about it," Veronica said, "the longer it may take. But that's something for you to work out. I'd say you're not doing too badly. Godfrey did ask you to the rehearsal, after all. And that's getting inside a bit further. The day may come, Tom, when you're inside without ever being quite sure how you got there. But by then perhaps you may not be thinking in those terms at all. At least, I hope so."

7

The Rehearsal

Moses Godfrey lived in Harlem. I got off the subway at 125th Street, and from there it was four blocks to his house. I had never been in Harlem during the daytime before. A couple of times, Mike and I had gone up to the Apollo Theater early in the evening. But it was all different in the daytime. I was so conscious of being white. Except for a cop and some storekeepers, all the faces I saw were dark. Nobody seemed to pay me any attention, but I felt like an alien. It was really like being in another country.

It sounds dumb, but until that afternoon, I'd never really thought about how split off New York City is. Split off by color. Oh, there are some Negroes in my neighborhood, but they're porters and delivery men. We don't even have Negro doormen—that's how "high class" our building is. And here I was in a city all by itself inside New York City. It was weird. And then it struck me that it must seem weird to a lot of these people when and if they ever walk in my neighborhood. How do they feel when all the faces they see are white? Man, talk about New York being integrated. It's a joke. Only ain't nobody laughing.

Godfrey lived in an old brownstone on Lenox Avenue. His place was on the first floor. A neatly typed card—MOSES GODFREY: BY INVITATION ONLY—was scotch-taped over his bell. I rang and Godfrey opened the door. He led me into a large room. It had a grand piano, the kind of deep, plush rug that made you imagine yourself in quicksand when you first stepped into it, and about a dozen wooden folding chairs. One whole wall was full of books. At a glance, nearly all of them seemed to be about Negro history. There was only one picture in the room—on top of the piano. It was of an old black man with a thicket of bristly white hair. He looked somewhat like the pictures I'd seen in the papers of new African leaders. He had a guitar in his hands and his eyes were those of a blind man. It was Big Charlie.

Godfrey said he'd be back, and disappeared into another room. While I was looking at the books, the musicians started to arrive. John Metcalf, the chunky drummer who always dressed as if he had an appointment with a photographer from *Esquire;* Sam Mitchell, the lanky, sour-looking tenor saxophonist; and Bill Hitchcock. Mary was with him, and just barely nodded to me. Bill introduced me to the other musicians.

"Will Burke's coming too," Hitchcock told me.

I was amazed. Burke is a trumpet player, white, and an old-timer. In the late thirties, he'd been considered pretty daring, but he hadn't worked much during the past ten years or so. I'd read that he'd been sick a long time, and then, when he got well, there had been very few jobs for a man who played the way he did. Burke couldn't make it anymore with the musicians with whom he used to work. Their styles were the same as they'd been twenty-five years ago. An easy, swinging beat, plenty of melody, and comparatively simple harmonies. Burke had gone beyond that, but yet he wasn't "modern" in the sense in which Moses Godfrey and his musicians were. He was in a kind of no-man's land. He had his own "bag"—you know, style—but it didn't fit with anyone else's.

I'd heard the only record Burke had made in the past few years, and it had sounded all jumbled up. His own horn playing was fine—it was like a man dancing. He had a skimming kind of beat, and on top of it he improvised very subtle ideas. What he did sounded simple at first, but when you listened to it closely, you heard how carefully he'd picked just the right notes out of a chord to say exactly what he had in mind. But what made the record bad was the rhythm section—it was just pounding away and not really listening to him. He could have been

59

in another town for all it would have mattered to them.

Anyway, Burke came in soon. He was about fifty, short, thin, and his crew cut was all white. There were deep lines in his forehead and around his mouth. He carried himself straight. Burke had never met any of Godfrey's musicians, and Hitchcock introduced him all around.

"I don't know why Moses asked me up," Burke said. "You guys are too hip for me." He smiled but the smile was more a nervous tic than a smile.

"You known Moses long?" Hitchcock asked.

"Twenty years maybe," said Burke. "We talk a lot from time to time, but we haven't played together much. He's *far* too hip for me."

"Depends on what you mean by hip." Godfrey had that habit of suddenly appearing when somebody was talking about him. He was smoking a pipe and had a batch of music manuscripts in his hand. Godfrey passed out the parts to each of the musicians. Burke looked at his and was puzzled. "There's hardly anything here, Moses," he said. "Just some chords. And a lot of space."

"The space is for you to fill in," Godfrey said. "You get a lot of freedom up here."

Sam Mitchell frowned at his part. "Look here, Moses." He pointed out a section of his part. "This horn can't make that. It is impossible to play those notes in sequence. Absolutely *im*possible."

Godfrey stared at him. "You a musician?"

"Oh, come on," said Mitchell.

"You a musician or have you just been jiving us?"

"But Moses—"

Godfrey turned his back on Mitchell and walked over to the piano. Mitchell, grumbling, began trying different fingerings on his saxophone, trying to get the notes under his hands.

"He"—Moses pointed to Burke—"is *the* man in this number. We'll run over what I've given you until you know it, and then you put it away. And when you put it away, you listen to him. Listen to what he's talking about it, and if you have anything to add to it, you put it right in. You dig?"

Nobody said anything. Hitchcock scratched his chin, a half-smile forming. Johnny Metcalf looked as confident as always. Mitchell was still trying to figure out how to play the sequence of notes he'd complained about to Godfrey. Mary had her head in one of Godfrey's books and didn't look up for a long time.

It took about an hour and a half for the musicians to master the arrangement. Burke hadn't played very much, softly improvising lines on the chords he'd been given, but very tentatively. Godfrey paid no attention to Burke, concentrating instead on his regular musicians. He spent the whole time on the written score. Sam Mitchell finally figured out a way to play the "impossible" passage, and, pleased with himself, he grinned broadly.

"You decided to be a musician, huh?" Godfrey said to him.

"Man, do you *have* to write so hard?" Mitchell grimaced.

"I *have* to write what I hear," Godfrey answered. "If you didn't work for me, Sam, you'd stay in the same groove all your life. I ought to charge you for being in my band."

"Moses Godfrey's College of Advanced Musical Knowledge," Mitchell said sarcastically.

"That's right, man. And I'm not sure you're going to graduate. Now, let's get down to the nitty-gritty." Godfrey turned to Will Burke. "Will, there's no title on this piece. What does it say to you so far?"

"I haven't really been listening to it that way, Moses," said Burke. "I've just been listening to how it's put together."

"Feel," said Godfrey. "Think back and feel."

Burke stood there for a few seconds, looked up at the ceiling, and then said, "Well, it sounds square, but it sounded to me like kids playing."

Godfrey was pleased. "That's why you're here. I

thought you'd pick up on that. O.K., tell it like it was when you were a kid. How it felt in the street. Who you liked and who bugged you. Bring in the cops and the teacher and your parents. Bring it all in. Tell it like it was. And you guys"—Godfrey looked around the room—"listen to hear if you recognize any of it and then put yourselves in. When you were kids. Sam, you were a kid once, weren't you?"

Mitchell pursed his lips. "I was born eighty-two years old, and I get younger every day. Except when I come up here. A day up here adds ten years to my life."

"Maybe you can be the cop," said Godfrey. He went to the piano, beat out the tempo, and the music started. It was the most extraordinary two hours of jazz I'd ever heard. At first, the background for Burke consisted almost entirely of Moses' score, now thoroughly absorbed by the musicians. As Burke, however, became more confident and played more and more personal improvisations, the other men gradually began to add their own ideas and feelings to the music. Building on Moses' score, they invented countermelodies to what Burke was playing and to each other's stories. It was like watching a group of exceptionally skilled weavers, collaborating on a complicated but strangely beautiful rug.

As Moses had wanted, the main story line was always set by Burke. His eyes closed, his cheeks puffed out, Burke made that trumpet speak. I mean there were times when it actually did talk—or rather—chuckle, snort, snarl, razz, rage, whimper, bray, and whisper. And he invented melody lines I'd never heard before, and yet once I did hear them, they sounded immediately familiar. Some soared and dipped like a long football pass. Others were like talking in the dark when you were supposed to be asleep.

By the fifth or sixth time Burke and the others had gone through the music, I'd started to remember places out of my own childhood that I hadn't thought about for years. And feelings.

One time Burke went way deep into blues and I was like stabbed by remembering the first time I thought of death—as it applied to *me*. I was about eleven and had been walking up a very high and long hill. About halfway up, it suddenly hit me that I wasn't going to live forever. I really wasn't. And then I wondered how many years I did have left, and I brooded about that off and on for a long time.

By half past six I was exhausted, just from the listening and the remembering and the reliving. The musicians themselves were absolutely beat. They were now slouching in their chairs, their spines touching the edge of their seats. Burke was still standing, shaking his head as if he were surprised, but not saying anything.

Only Godfrey seemed not to be tired. He was glowing, striding around the room, congratulating the musicians. I looked at Mary Hitchcock. She seemed to be in a daze. Godfrey stopped in front of her and passed his hand over her eyes. She looked up, startled, and then grinned.

"I was a little girl, Moses," she said. "Playing with dolls and watching my mother cook and getting to erase the blackboards in school. I was back down in Danville, Virginia."

"I was stealing fruit on the South Side of Chicago," Sam Mitchell said, smacking his lips as if he could taste what he'd gotten away with. "And cutting school to go to the movies."

Each musician had entered into his own flashbacks while improvising around Godfrey's backgrounds and Will Burke's trumpet. Now everyone appeared to be waiting for Burke to talk. He looked around, shook his head some more, sat down, and cried. The crying didn't last long. Embarrassed, Burke reached into his pocket for a cigarette. "First time I've cried, Moses, since I was maybe eight years old."

"It'll do you good," Godfrey said. "It would do anybody good. It's a crazy scene where men aren't supposed to cry, where 'big boys' aren't supposed to cry. Man, when you feel like crying, cry! Otherwise, it all gets pressed down inside you, and sooner or later you look as if you never got all your feelings out. You look like Sam."

"Lay off, Moses," said the tenor saxophonist. "I'm too mean to cry."

"That's what I'm talking about," Godfrey said. "Anyway, I got Will up here today and I got this music written to teach you guys something. You've all been getting so hip. Me too. We're getting to where we don't need chords anymore and we're getting to where we've been finding new ways of bending time. But I wasn't so sure we were remembering where it's all at. I was getting to where I couldn't hear you guys—as *you*. I'd rather hear you as your old sour self, Sam, than listen to how fast you can play that horn. All of you dig what I mean?"

Everyone nodded. "And you—" Godfrey turned to Will Burke—"you were the key ingredient. I needed something to keep these guys from slipping into their regular groove."

Burke began to pack up his horn.

"Will," said Godfrey, "we're going to record this. O.K.?"

"You mean you'd use me on one of your record dates? The critics will.think you're raiding old men's homes."

"Critics?" Godfrey laughed. "I don't read none of them. No, just one. When he says he's liked something I did, I get worried and play it back again. And when he doesn't like something at all, I feel fine, because I figure the piece must have something good in it."

Burke held out his hand and Godfrey took it in both of his. "Me and you, man," said Godfrey. I watched Mary Hitchcock out of the corner of my eye to see how she was taking all this integration. She was smiling. Until she caught my eye. Then she stuck her tongue out at me. But she didn't seem mad.

8

Middle Blues

Soon after I got home that evening, there was a call from Mike. He'd heard about a summer job in a jazz band playing at a resort in the Berkshires in Massachusetts. I'd have to fake my age, but otherwise, Mike said he was sure I was good enough for the band. I auditioned, made it, and got my father's permission, although my mother didn't agree until my father promised they'd ride up there every other week to see if I was still alive.

It was a fine summer. The band wasn't all that great. Half the guys were from Boston and the rest from New York and Connecticut. Except for me, they were all in college, majoring in all kinds of different things than music. And to me, it showed. I mean they played well enough technically but they seldom got all the way inside their horns. Not that I did, but I noticed that about the only times all summer some people would stop dancing and just stand and listen, was when I took a solo. By the end of August, I'd just about made up my mind. I'd finish my senior year in high school, and then I'd become a musician. Full-time.

The job ended a couple of weeks before any of us

had to go back to school. One of the guys from New York drove me back to the city and said he'd call me if he heard of any sessions going on before he went back to Yale. A couple of nights later, he did call and said to meet him on the lower East Side. I got there about nine thirty. It was a neighborhood of old, decaying buildings, used mostly for small businesses during the day.

Now it was dark and kind of frightening. The session was in the top floor of one of those buildings, a loft in which a painter, his wife, and their three kids lived. It was a huge place and when I got there, there were about six musicians already playing. The painter and his family, I was told, were still down on Cape Cod, and they let a couple of their musician friends use their place until they came back.

Except for the guy from Yale. I didn't know any of the musicians. He was white. All the rest were Negro. They just nodded when I came through the door and went on playing. It took me quite a while to begin to figure out what they were doing. They weren't playing any songs I'd heard before and they weren't using chords on which to improvise. It seemed to me they were letting the melodies and the rhythms decide where they were going to go next. Some of it made no sense to me at all. It was like six conversations going on in six different rooms. But they seemed to be enjoying themselves.

69

Finally I tried to sit in, but I just couldn't get my bearings, and dropped out again. The guy from Yale seemed to be making it all right, but I wasn't sure I could tell how you knew you were making it. For a couple of hours, I just listened. Then I tried again, but I still couldn't get with it. It was getting late anyway, so I got up to leave.

"So long, whitey," one of the Negro musicians said. "Maybe another time. You're still too tied up with the way jazz is *supposed* to be."

I had to say something, and I was very curious besides. "What do you guys think of Moses Godfrey?" I asked.

"Oh, he's O.K.—for his time," another of the musicians said. "We've gone beyond that. He's in the past, man. Like Louis Armstrong. And Miles Davis. And Beethoven." He laughed.

When I got home, my father asked me how the session had gone. "I'm old-fashioned," I said.

"At sixteen, going on seventeen?"

"At birth, maybe." He looked at me curiously, but he didn't ask anything more. And I went to bed. I dreamed I was walking up a hill, playing my horn, and suddenly, I had no breath left. Mary Hitchcock was at the top, and waved at me to follow her. She went around a corner, I followed, and fell down, down, down into a hole that had no bottom. And I woke up, still out of breath.

I called the Savoy the next day. Godfrey was out of town on a tour. I called Veronica's house and there was no answer. I didn't know what to do with myself, and that evening I took the subway downtown and just started walking around the Village. I walked by the Eighth Street Bookshop and saw Jessica inside.

She was talking to a clerk, a thin, ruler-straight Negro with glasses, who looked about twenty. Jessica waved me in. "Tom Curtis"—she nodded to me —"Frederick Godfrey." She nodded to the clerk. "Fred," she added, "is Moses' son."

Fred Godfrey winced as she said this, and I wondered why. Anyway, I was so surprised I just blurted out, "Man, that's a father to be proud of!"

"Really?" Fred said. He was very cool. "From what I hear, I gather my father is quite skillful at what he does. But jazz isn't an area in which I have any competence."

He'd said "jazz" as if he were talking about the ugliest, dirtiest spider in the world.

"You mean"—I couldn't stop myself—"you don't hear him play?"

"I have not lived with my father"—Fred's voice was now ice-cold—"since I was two. We see each other occasionally, but to use the argot, we are not in the same groove. I'm sorry, but there are other customers."

"You look like a fish in a store window," Jessica

71

said when he'd left. She giggled. "Close your mouth. He's real."

I made a face and Jessica laughed.

Jessica had arranged for us to have coffee with Fred when the bookstore closed in about an hour. While waiting, we walked across the street to a record store. A dozen of Moses Godfrey's most recent albums were in the window, grouped around a big picture of Moses. In the picture, he was scowling, almost as if he were looking across the street at his son.

"What's happening, baby?" said the clerk, a small, wiry Negro with a goatee.

"Anything new by 'Trane?" Jessica asked.

"No. There *is* a new one out, but the man"—he jerked his finger in the direction of the back of his store—"hasn't paid his bills for the last shipment. So, no credit. The man is in the wrong business. Peter, Paul, and Magoo ought to be in that window. Or Stanley Getz, The Dreamer. Anything but these bothersome truthful noises. Truth don't sell, baby."

I asked for a Cecil Taylor album, and the clerk raised his eyebrows. "Your friend is moderately advanced. I must say a few of the colonialists are showing remarkable interest in learning the speech patterns of us natives in the bush."

"Come off it," said Jessica. "Tom just met Fred Godfrey, and he's still figuring that one out."

"Nothing to figure," said the man behind the counter. "Young Fred is still looking for that magic cream that's going to turn him all white outside. He's already all white inside."

"I don't dig," I said.

"You don't understand, sir?" The clerk bowed gravely. "That black cat is ashamed of being black. He is ashamed that his father is black and that his father plays that black jazz. You ever hear of Jews changing their names and fixing their noses because they're ashamed of being Jews?"

I nodded.

"Well, sir, yonder Mr. Godfrey is in a bind. No point changing his name. His nose will pass. Even his hair is pretty straight. But that color, sir, will not rub away. Not all the ingested books of the Western world will chase that color away. It is a sad, sad tale and I am moved, sir, moved to vomit."

Jessica laughed, but I didn't know what to do. I figured the safest thing was to say nothing. "And you, sir"—he leaned toward me until the goatee almost brushed against my shirt—"I would bet that you dream of being black. You search for the magic cream too. Ah, if only you were black, you would stride into jazz, and Coltrane and Monk and Miles and Cecil and Moses Godfrey would whisper among themselves and genuflect and cry, 'The Savior is here. Let us all listen to his wonderful noise because he is the blackest of all.' "

"How did you know I played anything?" I asked. And then Jessica laughed so hard she bent over and put her hands on her stomach.

"You admit my hypothesis, sir," said the clerk. "How candid of you! Fate, Miss Jessica, is so cruel. This young man could have been the son of Moses, and gray Fred could have been the son of Nelson Rockefeller. Cruel, cruel, how cruel it all is. Maybe, sir, in the next life you will be born to one of the few sharecroppers left in Mississippi. And"—he raised his hand like a magician—"you will have your roots!"

I don't like to be made fun of, but I didn't know any way to get back at him, so I paid for the Cecil Taylor album and left. Jessica hurried after me. "He was just putting you on a little," she said.

"But why?" I said. "Why does everybody Negro have to have fun at my expense?"

"It's not every Negro. And besides, consider it part of your initiation. You do want to be on the inside?"

"But where do I get the passport?"

We walked down Eighth Street to Sixth Avenue. At the corner was a table and a sign: SUPPORT COFO —GIVE TO THE MISSISSIPPI PROJECT. On either side of the sign were pictures of Negroes who had been beaten in Mississippi for trying to register to vote. Sitting on chairs behind the table were a white boy about my age and a Negro girl about Mary Hitchcock's age.

"Hi, Jess," said the girl. "You free tomorrow?"

"What's happening?" Jessica asked.

"We're picketing a school on the lower East Side tomorrow. Principal there says Negroes and Puerto Ricans ought to be happy they're even let into his school."

"He was dumb enough to *say* that?" asked Jessica.

"Yeah. He was talking to a delegation from Downtown CORE and he blew his cool. So we're going to educate the educator." Jessica wrote down the time and place of the picketing and we started back to the bookstore.

Fred was waiting for us, and we walked down Eighth Street again to Riker's and ordered coffee.

"How's your sister?" Jessica asked.

"In San Francisco, married, in jail," Fred said kind of glumly.

"No kidding?"

"Yes, she got religion. Joined CORE out there and was arrested when they staged a sit-in at a bank. Thirty days."

"Does Moses know that?"

"I have no idea." Fred was suddenly angry. "I suppose you think that makes me the black sheep—sorry, the white sheep—of the family."

Jessica sipped her coffee.

"You're supposed to be a man first, right?" Fred spoke quickly, snapping out his words. "That's the whole idea of integration, right? Well, why can't I *be* myself without thinking black all day and all night? I want to teach philosophy. Is that a betrayal of 'my people?' Would having a Negro professor of philosophy at Harvard be such a bad thing? There's more than one way to advance the race."

"Is that why you're going to be a professor of philosophy—to advance the race?" Jessica asked.

"No, of course, not. My father loves jazz. That's his way of being himself and growing, right? Well, philosophy is just as important to me. No, I don't want to be a *Negro* professor of philosophy. I want to be a *valuable* professor of philosophy."

"So why did you tie it into race?"

"Because I'm on the defensive, that's why. I don't picket, I don't go down to Mississippi, I don't like jazz. So I'm an Uncle Tom. I'm supposed to be trying to get white. I'm a traitor. And so I get trapped anyway in being black. I have to keep justifying myself."

"I'm not saying this in judgment, Fred," said Jessica. "At least I'm trying not to. But why can't you move toward that professorship and be some part of 'the movement' too?"

"Because it's not my nature. Here I'm trying to be myself, and I know that I just *can't* go out there on the street and picket. I'd feel phony. I'm not denying the value of what 'the movement' is doing, but that's just not the route for me. Same thing about going down to Mississippi. I'm not the type. Maybe I'm simply a coward. But I *know* I couldn't stand being beaten. And if I was beaten, I'd hit back, and I'd be dead. What's the point? I don't want to be a martyr. I—I'm trying to make my contribution by being myself. Don't you see any of that at all?"

"You mean when the society's integrated, you'll be there as one of the first models?" Jessica said.

"There's no point." Fred looked into his coffee. "Nobody understands. Look. My father. He's never been on a picket line. He's never been in Mississippi. Why is he immune from criticism?"

"Your father," said Jessica, "is saying his thing through music. If you'd listen to him, you'd know how *much* he's saying about what it's like to be Negro, about what his—and your—heritage is, about the pride as well as the pain in it. Ugh, I sound like one of those new 'sociological' jazz critics."

"And I'm betraying that heritage, huh? Because I don't respond to jazz. Because I don't pat my feet? Because I don't have that 'natural' rhythm? Talk about stereotypes! Can't a Negro choose his own way even if it's different from what's gone before?"

"You have scored a point, Fred," Jessica said, getting up. "At least I think you have. I wonder what your father would say."

"I don't ask the advice of a man who left two kids when one was two and the other three."

"And he's never volunteered any?"

"All he ever says by way of advice is that every tub has to sit on its own black bottom."

"What's that mean?" I finally said something.

"It means"—Fred looked at me—"what the Greeks said. Know thyself. It means no one else can tell you who you are. No one else can sit where you're sitting."

"Well," said Jessica, "you seem to be pretty straight on that score."

"Yes," said Fred, "but the Greeks didn't add that you still have to pay dues even when you know you're right."

"Pay dues?" Jessica said with a slight smile.

"Oh, I know the language. You know, when a Jew gets out of college, nobody expects him to sound like a dialect comedian. But if you're Negro and

don't talk hip, then you're a Tom. Reverse stereotypes again."

"Color is sure complicating," Jessica said. "Take
Tom, here. He wants to be a jazz musician."

Fred laughed for the first time, a grating kind of
laugh. "Welcome to the club." He held out his hand
to me. "The outsiders."

I took his hand—although I didn't want to.

9
Lumps in the Pudding

By Christmas, things were looking up. A little. My grades in school were good enough so that if I did decide to go to college, I'd probably get in at least one of the places my father preferred. I really didn't have any particular choice as long as the college was near to where there'd be some jazz to hear and some musicians to play with. I still wasn't at all sure whether I would go to college, but I'd applied to a few places anyway.

More important—to me—was that our band was working into shape and my own playing was getting a lot more free. Mike kept saying I was ready to record, and that I ought to send a tape to Blue Note or one of the other jazz companies. But I didn't take that seriously. People who don't play tend to be more enthusiastic than people who know what's really going on—and what *isn't* happening—in the music. What did make me feel good was that a few times during a solo I'd be taking, Tim, the piano player, would look at me kind of surprised. We usually didn't talk much. I'd wanted to tell him I'd gotten to know Moses Godfrey, but I figured he'd think I was bragging. Besides, I wanted to keep those conversations with Godfrey to myself for a while. I didn't even tell Mike much about them. Anyway, once Tim came over after a rehearsal.

"Somebody in your family die or something?" he said.

"What do you mean?"

"You're not just fooling with that horn anymore. You sound like you've had some experiences that aren't in the exercise books."

"I've had some problems." I was embarrassed. I didn't want to go into that whole color thing with him and my uncertainty about whether I could ever really be what I wanted to be. I still remembered how bugged he'd been when I'd asked him to bring a Negro friend to a rehearsal.

"Well," said Tim, "I wish you more problems. Nothing fatal, you understand. But you're beginning to sound like you know nothing's simple."

"That's the truth." I felt I'd been greatly complimented.

"Yeah." Tim started to go. "Want to know my philosophy?"

I nodded.

"It's like that Irish writer James Stephens said: 'There's always lumps in the pudding.' But some puddings do taste better than others."

I didn't tell Tim another reason I was getting to

play better was that I had started taking lessons from Bill Hitchcock once a week. I guess I wanted Tim to think I'd done it all by myself. And insofar as the emotional part of it was concerned, I had. My head was full of questions and confusions and uncertainties; and somehow the only way I could get any release was by telling about all those doubts—and all the things I wanted to become—in music. So I was telling stories all the time, and they were all mine. None of them had any endings yet, though.

The lessons were important too, though. I used most of my allowance to pay for them, along with what I earned working occasional dance dates with our band. "I don't like to teach," Bill had said when I'd asked about a regular series of lessons. "I have so much to learn myself, it doesn't make sense for me to come on as any kind of expert. But I do begin to hear something in you and I'm curious as to what's down there. So we'll see how it works out." Godfrey showed up once in a while during my lessons, but never said anything.

Bill taught me some of the ways in which the younger jazz musicians were moving away from chords and even from a regular beat. "There are a lot of different ways to swing," Bill told me at the end of one lesson soon after the series had started. "In his way, Bach was a swinger. And Beethoven was. Listen to his Seventh Symphony. And in jazz, the old guys from New Orleans swung in one way, the Harlem musicians used to swing in another, Charlie Parker found *his* way, and so it keeps going.

"Now, you read some of the critics and they'll tell you that it isn't jazz unless you can tap your foot to it. That's nonsense. The thing is whether you can *feel* a pulse when you're listening. It doesn't have to be pounding· in your ears all the time like a drill. Listen carefully to Charlie Mingus. His is another way. His beat is like a curve, winding in and out, slowing down, speeding up. It's alive! And it's him! That's what counts—finding your own way of feeling time. And then finding guys who have a similar way."

Mary would sit in on the lessons once in a while, not saying anything. She was still cool to me but I didn't feel the anger that was there before, and once in a while, she acted as if I had some possibility of becoming a human being. Just before Christmas, on a rainy night, she said I could stay for dinner if I wanted to. As I called home and said I'd be late, two other guests arrived. One was Sam Mitchell, as sour-looking as ever, and the other was Dick Winters, a trumpet player who'd been with Larry Wilson's band as long as I could remember. Wilson had one of the last big jazz bands, and in order to survive, the band was on the road most of the year. It played college dances, what few ballrooms were left, private parties, and once had even been booked for the opening of a supermarket in a Negro neighborhood in Chicago.

"This boy"—Bill introduced me to Winters—"wants to be a jazz musician."

"Ain't there nothing else you can do?" Winters said with a grin. He was a burly man of about forty-five with graying hair. "It ain't all kicks, you know."

"That's the truth," said Mitchell, sinking onto the couch.

"You're going to bust all his balloons." Mary came in with the silverware. Their living room was also the dining room and Bill's practice area. "He thinks it's all glamor out there."

"Oh, I know it isn't easy," I said, not wanting to appear a total innocent. "I mean it takes a long time to get established and you have to travel a lot."

"Do you know what a *lot* of traveling is?" Winters leaned forward. "Do you know what it's like to spend ten years on a band bus, with kids back home who know the characters they see on television better than they know you? Have you any idea of what it's like to do a string of one-nighters by finishing a gig at two in the morning, piling into the bus and trying to sleep while the other guys are playing cards or telling jokes, and then coming into the next town just in time to get a fast, lousy sandwich and get on the stand where you're supposed to be full of energy and good spirits because you're being paid for *entertaining* those people?" He sighed heavily. "Boy, you get to where just the sight of a road map gives you the blues."

I was trying to sympathize with what they were saying, but the road just didn't seem that much of a drag to me. It sounded exciting. At least you didn't see the same old faces and the same old streets every day.

"That boy is listening so polite," Mary broke in, "I don't think your message is getting through."

Winters lit a cigar, leaned over, and poked his finger at me. "Every man has the right to go to hell his own way. And if you really got this thing in your blood, ain't nobody going to talk you out of it."

"Tell me," I said, "would *you* rather have done something else?"

Winters didn't answer for what seemed like a long time. "Well," he finally said, "I can't say it's all been bad. There have been kicks, and I did get to be a pretty good musician." Sam Mitchell made a mock bow to Winters. "But I'll tell you, I would have liked to try something that didn't leave me so vulnerable."

"Vulnerable?" I asked. "I don't understand."

"The critics, boy. Those guys who can't tell a C chord from a jet plane but who can affect how much your records sell. It's worse than that, though. When you write about a jazz musician, you're writing about his whole life. If you put him down out of no knowledge of who he is and what he's saying, you're like wiping out his life."

"But why pay attention to them?" I asked. "Godfrey doesn't."

"Moses," said Winters, "is cooler than I am. I can't *help* reading them. Especially that Irving Weston, because he's *everywhere*. Not only in *Down Beat*. Man, you pick up a magazine on plucking chickens, and there's an article by Weston on how chicken pluckers can learn to like jazz."

"Why are you so bugged with him?" Mary asked.

"I was on the bus"—Winters grimaced—"out of Wichita, Kansas, at three in the morning. I couldn't sleep, so I picked up *Down Beat*. And there was Weston, writing about a record I was on and saying I should have gone into another line of work. That I just didn't have it as a jazz musician. You know I almost cried. Me, going on fifty, and I almost cried because of what that white square said about me."

I almost felt like crying myself for a second. I could see Winters on that bus reading the review. But he hadn't scared me yet about the jazz life. I

86

figured I'd be like Godfrey and never read the critics.

As Mary started to serve the food, Mitchell turned to Winters. "No matter what you say—and I agree with it all—there are lots of worse jobs. Like having somebody sit on you in an office or having some machine come along and do what you're doing a hundred times better and faster."

"I'm not talking about no office job," Winters said impatiently. "This kid is young enough to be a doctor or a lawyer or something like that."

"But," Bill interrupted, "what kind of life is it if you don't like what you're doing?"

"How does he know he's going to like being out there as a jazz musician?" Winters came close to shouting. "What I'm saying is he ought to get more things going for him than just music. He's young, man. Let him learn to do something else too, so that if he decides the life isn't for him, he isn't stuck on that slide going nowhere."

"I remember a cat," Mitchell said softly, "who used to be with Duke. Trombone player. He was about twenty-eight, and he'd always wanted to be a lawyer. All he read were books about the law. And I used to say to him, 'You're only twenty-eight. You got some college credits. Take five or six years of whatever it takes, and you'll be a lawyer.' 'No,' he kept saying, 'I'm too old.' So now he's a lot older, and he's *still* a trombone player somewhere. Me, like the kid here, I never wanted to be anything else. But if you got doubts, hedge your bet, boy."

"*Do* you have doubts?" Mary asked me.

I didn't know how to answer that. I didn't have any doubts that jazz was what I wanted, but I did have doubts that I could make it in jazz. And that's what I told them.

"Nobody can write you out insurance on that," Bill said. "Who can tell a novelist or a painter he's going to make it? Anything you want that's worth having, you got to take a chance on."

"Well," said Mitchell, grinning, "we're wasting talk. Twenty years from now, that boy will be coming into a club to see you and he'll be a big, rich lawyer or something like that."

"It's too soon to tell." Bill shook his head.

"Yes," said Mary, "that boy could surprise us. And himself. So Moses says, anyway."

"Yeah," Mitchell guffawed, "but Moses ain't much of a prophet. He once told me his own son was going to help change the world."

"Maybe he will," Mary said.

"You don't change nothing by running away from it," Mitchell answered; and I said it was time for me to leave.

10

The Critic

In December the album Godfrey had recorded with Will Burke came out. It was called *Street Games,* and the first reviews were all bad. The critics wrote as if they were computers that somebody had programmed. Almost all of them said that there was a clash of styles, and you couldn't get anything of value out of mixing old players like Burke and modern musicians like Godfrey.

One night, outside the Savoy, I asked Godfrey how he'd felt about the reviews. He stroked his head, rubbed his back against the door, and said, "Like I told you, I don't read but one of them, the very worst one. But a man always has friends," he chuckled, "who'll be sure to tell him about the bad reviews. I wasn't surprised. They weren't feeling the music. They came to it with their minds already made up. As if there's a book of answers in jazz, and all you have to do is look up what's never been tried before and you just say that kind of thing is *impossible.*"

It was a slow night, and Godfrey had told the owner he was going to take an hour between sets. He wanted to see Burke, who lived in an old tenement around the corner from the Savoy. The entrance door of the building was scarred all over, and nearly every pane of glass in it was broken. The hall smelled so bad I almost gagged. "Being a landlord," said Godfrey as we walked up the stairs, "is like being in charge of the next war. Landlord lives in some fine pad and sends a man around to collect his bread. He never smells this and *he's* got hot water all the time. Cat who starts the next war just pushes a button. Only thing different is he'll get his too. But maybe not. He'll probably push that button from way deep down in some shelter."

Burke was on the fourth floor. He had a small room with a bed, a table, two chairs, an old upright piano, his horn, some music manuscript paper, and a dozen paperback books. There was also a cardboard wardrobe and a hot plate. His refrigerator, I could see, was the ledge outside his window where a bottle of milk and some cans of beer were standing.

I looked around for a record player, but couldn't see any. Not even a radio. Burke guessed what my curiosity was about. "I'm like Moses," he said. "I'd rather hear music live. Once it gets into a can, it's over for me. It's the process—the making of it— more than the result, in a way, that gets me."

Burke sat on the bed. Godfrey and I took a chair. We talked about the record and the mistakes

Burke insisted he had found in his own work. "I did hear *that* record." He turned to me. "Couldn't resist it. Went to a friend of mine who has a phonograph. I should have done another take, Moses."

"They weren't mistakes." Godfrey balanced himself back and forth on the chair. "I know. You hear some other notes now that might have been just a little more right than some of the ones you played, but you're old enough to know that when it gets perfect, it ain't human. Best stories I ever heard—in music or out of it—had some imperfections. A *good* storyteller takes those rough edges and lets them lead him into some place he might not have found otherwise. Time enough for the machines to take over all of music. I hear a mistake, as you call it, and I know the music's breathing."

After a while Godfrey decided he wanted some coffee, and since Burke didn't have any left, we went out. We walked down to Second Avenue and as we turned the corner, we saw two young hoods working over a Puerto Rican. There wasn't a cop in sight and maybe twenty-five people stood around, looking. No one made a move to stop it. The Puerto Rican was down on the sidewalk now, and the other two were kicking him.

A thin Negro rushed in, shouting, "Let him alone!" It was Fred Godfrey. I heard his father gasp,

"I'll be damned." The hoods turned on Fred and he fell—deliberately, it seemed—on top of the Puerto Rican so that he would absorb the blows.

I yelled, "Cops!" and the hoods ran away. There still weren't any cops around, but I'd thought the trick was worth a try. The Puerto Rican seemed O.K., but Fred was shaking. He couldn't stop. He was like a puppet with someone shaking the strings as hard as he could.

We led Fred into a cafeteria, and once he was able to sip some coffee, he calmed down a little.

"Surprised?" Fred said to his father. "So am I." He sounded bitter.

Godfrey didn't seem to know what to do. I felt uncomfortable watching him put out his hand, as if to touch Fred, and then drawing it back.

"But I'm still a Tom, right?" Fred's voice was harsh and loud. "I mean, a Puerto Rican doesn't count, does he? It should have been a black man, right?"

"Fred," said Godfrey, "I'm not your judge. If you want to know what I think, you did the right thing."

Fred didn't answer, finished his coffee, paid for it, and left. Nobody said anything for a while. Godfrey was staring into his cup and Burke was shaking his head slowly from side to side. I wanted to say something to make Godfrey feel better, but I couldn't think of anything.

"Time to go back." Godfrey motioned in the direction of the Savoy and we started moving there. "His mother," Godfrey said as we walked, "didn't think jazz was 'respectable,' let alone for a Negro. She wanted me to go work in the post office, and there was nothing I could do but leave. She wouldn't change and I knew I couldn't. He and his sister, though, never understood it that way. They think that since I left them, I couldn't have had any feeling for them. And they've never forgiven me, especially since I hardly got to see them all those years I was on the road.

"If it is true, like some of the hippies say, that Fred has been trying to be white all his life—and I'm not sure it is—that's because of me. He wanted to be as different from his father as he could. Some of that's natural, of course. Any boy with any spirit has to try to be different in some way. But Fred went at it like a scientific project. If he could, he'd have three arms because I have two."

"What he did there"—Burke looked back—"is getting to be a pretty rare thing."

"Yeah. If he could stop fighting me, or what he thinks of as being me, he'd be a very straight kid. He didn't seem hurt to you, did he?"

"No," said Burke. "It was shock. He'd shocked himself. Now he's got to think about it."

"Well—" Godfrey put his hand on my shoulder,

the first time he'd ever touched me. "Like I told you, there's no place as full of surprises as New York."

Sam Mitchell was leaning against the window when we got to the Savoy. He had a strange kind of smile on his face, like he was anticipating being mean. "We got royalty tonight, Moses." He gestured inside.

"Like who?"

"The king of the critics, man. Irving Weston himself. In person. Not a magazine. Not a book. The man himself."

Godfrey suddenly had the same look as Mitchell. "Well," he said slowly, "we must make him feel at home."

"Moses"—Burke stood in front of him—"it's not worth it."

"Why, whatever do you mean, Will? I am just going to respond to his vibrations. He will choose the game."

"That's just what I was afraid of," said Burke. Godfrey and the musicians went in, and I used my own entrance. For the past few months, I'd been allowed to come in through the kitchen door and stand in the kitchen, watching and listening to the music.

I rushed to look out into the club. I'd caught some of Burke's fear that some kind of embarrassing scene was going to happen, but at the same time,

I was looking forward to it. And I was curious about Weston. I'd been reading him for a long time, but I'd never seen him. Except for pictures on the back of his books on jazz. He wrote like he was God. I mean, there were almost never any qualifications in what he wrote. If he liked a musician, the guy was the greatest. If he didn't, he came down hard.

There he was at a table. Short and kind of pudgy. The pictures had only shown his head. He wore a beard, but while it looked fierce in the pictures, it seemed kind of pasted on when you saw him. He was sitting with three friends, and although the intermission trio was playing, he never stopped talking. When the trio finished, Godfrey's men began to get on the stand. As usual, one by one, each at his own pace. Godfrey was the last. He strolled down the aisle, acknowledging none of the greetings he received, sat down at the piano, and immediately kicked off the first number.

Weston kept talking although he occasionally did look up at the musicians and write something in a notebook on the table. Sam Mitchell plunged into a solo, and as he got louder the conversation at the front table got louder. Suddenly, Godfrey gave the musicians a cut-off sign. They stopped instantly, and the room was silent except for Weston's harsh voice: "—so I told him you're not going to get *me* to do a liner note for any seventy-five dollars. For *my* name on a record, the price starts at two hundred." Weston realized what was happening, turned around, reddened, and started scribbling furiously.

Godfrey, his face impassive, continued to sit there. Mitchell was trying very hard not to laugh and the other musicians were grinning broadly. There must have been a full minute more of silence until Godfrey, turning slightly in Weston's direction, asked coolly, "May we continue?"

"Sorry," Weston muttered, and the music began again. I felt like cheering. For the rest of the number, Weston was rigidly attentive. His eyes never left the musicians, even when he wrote something down. By the third number, the tension in the club that had been created by Godfrey's lesson in manners had evaporated. About half the people were listening closely, but the rest of them were immersed in conversation and even Weston occasionally made some comment to his friends.

Godfrey began " 'Round Midnight." The arrangement started with just him on piano. He hunched over, closed his eyes, and played very softly. He was extending the melody, not just paraphrasing it, and it was as if he were about to create an entirely new song. Because he was playing so softly, the talk in the room became very obvious; and although some of the talkers soon lapsed self-consciously into silence, there were two tables at which the conversation continued, making it very difficult to hear everything Godfrey was improvising. I wanted to yell at them to keep quiet, but then I'd have been banished from my place in the kitchen.

Godfrey stopped, pulled the microphone over to him, and still sitting, he looked into the room and said, "Why *do* you come here? Because it's hip to come on as if jazz meant something to you? Because you get kicks out of watching someone do an emotional striptease? What do you think I'm doing up here? If I wanted to play for myself, I'd stay in my room. I'm trying to be straight with you, to tell you what I'm feeling. And when you listen, I get back something from you. *When* you listen. Now, if you don't want to hear what I'm saying, go someplace else. But if you come in here, you got to do some work too. I got better things to do than play background music for your drinking and talking. Why don't you all go home and put on the radio? And some records too. Then you'll *not* be hearing even more."

Godfrey got up, walked off the stand, down the aisle to the kitchen, past me into the street, and I followed him. I felt like cheering. The owner, a tall, fat man who usually stayed behind the bar, started to come after Godfrey, but Sam Mitchell stopped him.

"If you want him to come back, friend, leave him

be." Mitchell returned to the stand, kicked off another number, and the band played without a pianist. The owner, scowling, went back behind the bar.

Outside, Godfrey leaned against the window, staring into space. I knew him well enough by now not to talk to him. Besides, talk wasn't necessary. I was sure he knew I understood what had happened and was on his side. A few minutes later, Weston came out. "Look here," he said to Godfrey, "I admit I was rude at the start of the set, but what you did is a lot ruder. There are a lot of people in there who aren't talking, who did want to hear you. Why punish them?"

Godfrey didn't move and didn't say a word.

Weston was exasperated. "Besides, did it ever occur to you that if what you were saying were strong enough, it would cut through conversation and *make* that conversation die down? I never heard Charlie Parker tell an audience to be quiet."

By now I was so mad at Weston that I wanted to get into it too, but as I started to open my mouth, Godfrey shook his head at me. "Some fine day, boy" —he spoke to me as if Weston wasn't there—"I'm going to come by where Mr. Weston writes and I'm going to jabber while he types. And some fine night, I'm going to come by where he's alone with a girl, and I'm going to jabber some more."

The owner came out on the sidewalk. "Can we expect the pleasure of your company later this evening?" he asked Godfrey. "I got to make some kind of announcement to those people who paid to hear you."

"They heard me."

"They didn't pay for a sermon," said the owner.

"Then they got a bargain."

"Look, are you coming back or aren't you?"

Godfrey laughed. "You'd really like to fire me, wouldn't you? You'd like to kick me out, and have a picture of it too so you could look at it and get kicks from it any time you wanted to. But I draw, don't I? I do more business for you than anybody else. So you're waiting on me even though you can't stand me. You're in a trap, man. A trap baited with bread."

The owner got so red in the face he looked as if he might actually burst.

"Now I'm going to tell you what to do," Godfrey said. "You go back and you tell them it is the policy of the house that the musicians are not to be disturbed. You tell them that if they can at least keep quiet—I'm not asking them to *really* listen, because it's too late for most of them—I will be there for the next set. You going to do that?"

The owner started to say something, shook his

head hard, and walked back in. We could hear him making an announcement about Godfrey coming back if they'd please keep quiet.

"He makes it sound like I'm begging." Godfrey frowned. "But no matter. One lesson at a time."

"Well, I'm not coming back," said Weston. "I've had enough temperament for one night. And don't think I'm not going to write about this!"

"I'm scared, Mr. Weston. I'm so scared, I might just shine your shoes if you'd ask me. Or maybe I could come by and take out your garbage."

"Moses." Will Burke had joined us. "Let's take a walk. Save it, man. You only got so much energy. Save it for the music."

"I was right to start with." Godfrey took Burke by the elbow. "I had a policy for a long time of not talking to people. Most people. No way to communicate. Nobody listens." They walked away.

Weston stood there and muttered. "He thinks he's so special."

I took a good look at Weston and *he* didn't look so special. Not to me.

11
Playing the Game

Jessica came home from college for the Christmas holidays. She'd started her first year at Radcliffe. On Christmas Eve she called and invited me over for the next day. "It's open house. Actually, it's been open house here since yesterday and it looks as if it'll go on until at least July fourth. So come any time."

I came by around two in the afternoon. In the living room a Duke Ellington record was playing while Veronica listened with her eyes closed, Jessica read, and Sam Mitchell sprawled in a chair, looking at the ceiling.

From the next room came the hard, clipped sounds of ping-pong. When I walked in, Godfrey was moving around his end of the table as if he had six hands. At the other end was George Dudley, a trombonist who led his own combo and had been very successful in the past couple of years. He had first become widely known for his "soul" music—a mixture of modern jazz harmonies with the beat of old-time Negro gospel music and simple gospel-type melodies. He still capitalized on the soul kick, but he also occasionally played the fairly advanced jazz he preferred.

Dudley was tall, skinny, and terribly cool. He was known for not displaying emotion on stand, and I could see he was the same way when he wasn't working. He seemed to hardly move but he was more than holding his own against Godfrey. Calm and careful, he appeared able to anticipate almost every one of Godfrey's shots, and he made his own points not by slamming the ball but by slicing it with soft accuracy just beyond Godfrey's reach.

As Dudley went ahead Godfrey began to puff and mutter. "Man, you're too scientific. Playing with you is like playing with a machine."

"Conservation of energy is my bag," Dudley drawled. "Why waste it?"

Godfrey blasted the ball, and Dudley stepping far back somehow managed to return it, and besides, made the return look easy.

"Ain't nobody can stay as cool as you for so long." Godfrey was breathing heavily. "Someday you're just going to explode."

"I wouldn't worry about it, Moses." And Dudley won another point.

In the other room, Mary and Bill Hitchcock had arrived along with Will Burke and Fred Godfrey. Moses' son heard his father from the ping-pong room but made no move to go in. He started talking to Veronica. After a while, Jessica proposed a game,

Born Again. "We'll go around the room and each of us will tell what we would like to be if we could be born again. It's no fun unless you tell the truth, no matter how outrageous."

It seemed like a pretty square game to me, and I didn't pay too much attention. While they played, I went through a new batch of records Veronica had bought, reading the liner notes and wishing I could afford to own the albums. There wasn't a clinker in the lot. When Godfrey and Dudley came back into the room, I put down the records. I wondered if they were going to play the game.

Jessica pointed at Godfrey and said, "Quickly, without thinking, what would you want to be if you could be born again?"

"I pass." Godfrey smiled. "I'm not much for what could have been."

"You!" she was pointing at me. I hadn't thought to prepare an answer and I blurted out, "I'd be born again as Moses Godfrey." Everybody but Godfrey and his son laughed. I flushed.

"Wouldn't *anyone* black do?" Mary Hitchcock asked.

"I didn't mean it that way." I was angry now. "And besides, I don't think of Moses as a Negro anymore."

"Anymore?" Mary said acidly.

"Well, I guess I did, at first. But I mean the *way* he is. He's his own man."

"You give up already on being *your* own man?" Godfrey asked.

"No, no. Look, I was just playing the game."

Dudley was silent for a few seconds. When he spoke, his voice was low and hard. "I'd have been a king. An African king. And maybe back there one of my ancestors *was* a king. Anyway, I'd be a king back around the sixteenth century. Or earlier. A king who sent people all over the world to learn what was worth learning about everywhere. And that way, I'd have had the latest in weapons so that when those Europeans came, we'd have wiped them out. And the generations after me would have wiped them out. And while the Europeans, and later the Americans, were fighting and killing each other, we'd keep building the most civilized society in the world. We'd just use weapons for defense."

"What about those African kings that sold other Africans as slaves?" Fred Godfrey asked.

"The first ones caught doing that," Dudley went on, "would have been so horribly punished, no one else would ever have tried."

"What about now?" Jessica said. "How could you defend yourself against atom bombs and, for that matter, against fallout from atom tests?"

"Since we didn't have to waste our resources in

fighting for anything but defense, we'd have long since perfected defenses against that too. Maybe a dome covering the whole continent. A dome nothing could get through. We'd grow all our own food, manufacture everything we need, and let the rest of the world go to hell."

"So that's who you are." Moses got up and stretched.

"What do you mean?" Dudley was annoyed.

"Even in your fantasies," Moses answered, "you build walls around yourself. That's why your music is so cold. You really run scared all the time."

I felt a chill. Everybody was like frozen, looking at Godfrey and Dudley. I was afraid. I didn't know what was going to happen, but I knew *something* was going to happen.

"I stay whole, man." Dudley's voice rose and became harsh. "Ain't nobody gets to me I don't want to let in. I stay in control. That's why I don't need your integration." He looked at Jessica. "I don't go where I'm not wanted and I don't let anybody I don't want bother with me."

"They really got you, George," said Godfrey. "They *de*humanized you."

"He sounds pretty human to me." Sam Mitchell laughed. "At least the humans I know. Only difference from most of us is that he's making it."

"It's like walking around in a suit of armor." Godfrey shook his head. "You're so limited all the time in where you can move. Can't be much kicks in that. I tell you, listen to his music. Ain't never any flesh and bones in it."

Dudley had risen. "I don't have to make speeches to an audience, Moses, to make them listen."

"Sure, you don't. Because you're not telling them anything they don't want to hear. You're giving them candy all the time."

"Are you saying I sell out?"

"No, man, it's worse than that. You got nothing to sell out. You've played it safe so long you're just like most of *them*. Any time now you'll be going on the Ed Sullivan show. You're empty, man. Cool and empty."

Dudley suddenly hit Godfrey in the mouth. We all looked as the blood ran down Godfrey's beard. Nobody moved.

"There's some hope yet," said Godfrey as he wiped the blood off with his handkerchief. "You want to do it again?"

I thought I heard Dudley swallow a sob, but his face was like stone as he walked out of the room and out the front door.

12
The Freest Night Club in the World

For the next few weeks I kept arguing with myself about whether I'd go on to college next year. Mike came up with what seemed to me to be a sensible idea. "Why don't you cool it for a year?" he said. "You've still got plenty of time. See how it feels trying to make it in jazz for a while."

I tried the idea on my father and he didn't put it down. "That's a possibility," he agreed. "There's something to the theory that youngsters ought to know a little more about life before they go on to college. Although you seem to have been learning a few things these nights with Mr. Godfrey and your other friends. Anyway, you don't have to decide right now."

Meanwhile, I was feeling better and better about my music. It was hard to wait between sessions of our band, and the lessons with Bill Hitchcock also couldn't come soon enough. Most of what happened in between the times I was playing music just didn't seem entirely real. Other guys in my class were getting hung up on girls. I went out with some and liked it, but I was hung on my horn.

One afternoon I was so eager to get to Hitchcock's,

I got there too early. As I was about to knock I heard a trumpet. Just the trumpet. No piano. It's hard enough to put music into words, and actually I don't think you can do it with any real sense of that other language of sound, but describing *that* trumpet is especially hard.

The trumpet chilled me, for one thing. Where Dizzy Gillespie, even when he's playing the blues, sounds as if he's bursting with life, as if he really digs life, this trumpet sounded as if it hadn't made up its mind at all. There seemed to be a constant battle going on between the blackest blues feelings on the one hand and defiance on the other. In between, clashing against each other, were rage and yearning and mocking and very quick moments of peace. At least that's the way it sounded to me. I can't begin to tell you what he was doing technically, because I'm not sure, but he was getting sounds out of that horn—human sounds—I'd never heard before. It was like several men talking, demanding, praying, yelling, whispering, and cursing.

Finally I did knock, and when I walked inside, I saw a small, thin Negro of about twenty. He wore horn-rimmed glasses, a red corduroy shirt, chino pants, and sneakers. He looked familiar, but I couldn't remember where I'd seen him before. It was as if he was reading my mind, because he stuck out his hand and said, "The loft." He was one of the musicians I'd tried to ·sit in with at the end of the summer and hadn't been able to get with at all.

"Tom Curtis, Danny Simmons." Bill made the introductions. Now I remembered the name too. I'd read in *Down Beat* that he'd made his first album, but I hadn't connected the name with the trumpet player in the loft.

Simmons put his horn in his case and started to leave, but Hitchcock said, "You can stick around if you want to."

"Yeah, I'd like that," said Simmons. "No heat in my place. The landlord disappeared, and so we're on a rent strike, but that doesn't fix a furnace that ought to be in the Smithsonian Institute; and in that whole building, there isn't nearly enough bread to buy a new one. So, thank you. I'll soak up some more heat."

Simmons sat through my lesson without saying anything. I was very curious to know more about him, though, and when the lesson was over, I invited him to have some coffee with me. We went into a restaurant on the next block, and to start things off, I asked how his album was doing.

"Doing? You mean selling?" Simmons laughed. "If it sells a thousand copies, everybody will be surprised—me most of all. The guy who made it is smart, though. His catalogue doesn't have much of the 'new thing.' You know, the kind of music you heard us making in the loft that night. Fifteen years ago he got caught with very little of what Charlie Parker and Dizzy were doing, and until he began recording boppers fast, he lost some bread as modern jazz became moderately popular. He doesn't want to get hung up again, so even though he doesn't like or understand what I'm doing, he's taking a chance." Simmons gulped down his coffee and went on: "It's not that much of a chance. He paid us all scale because he knows I need a record out more than he needs to put it out right now. And I'm supposed to get three percent royalty on all the sales, but that means like three dollars and a quarter in the next five years."

"Where are you working?"

"You really don't know what's happening, do you?" said Simmons. "If Ornette Coleman isn't working regularly and George Russell isn't and Cecil Taylor isn't, how can I get a gig? Oh, if I pushed hard, maybe I could catch on with some rhythm and blues band or maybe even with somebody like Art Blakey, but there's no place for me to play *my* music. You heard what we were doing in the loft? Man, that would drive any night club owner I know up the wall. Even those hippie disc jockeys on FM are afraid to play my record. Maybe I'm kidding myself when I say 'afraid.' They don't understand it. They don't think it's jazz. Man, they hate it."

"But suppose you went with Blakey, you'd still have practice time for yourself and you'd get more of a name and an income too."

"You don't dig. You just don't dig. Look, if I go with Blakey or anybody who's established enough to have any work, I'd have to play *his* way. I've been through that. I've been playing since I was fourteen. I've been in funky blues bands on the South Side of Chicago, I've been house pianist in a club where just everybody passed through for a week or two, and I even accompanied some singers. It was a good thing. I learned a lot. But when I started to get myself together and find out what *I* wanted to say, I had to stop playing for other people. Otherwise I'd be split in two. You can't lay down on a job. The leader's paying you, you've got to put out for him. So where would the energy be for my own thing when I'd be done?

"I mean you get through at three in the morning, and you got to unwind. You've been trying to find different things to say all night, your mind's racing, you're hung up on things you should have played better and notes you shouldn't have played at all. And it isn't even your music, man. So by the time you do unwind, hang out a while with some friends, have something to eat and maybe read the paper, it's seven or eight in the morning. You get up at three or four in the afternoon, and by the time you really wake up and get things done like taking the laundry in or whatever, it's time to eat and time to hit for the first set around nine thirty. And then, if you're working with a leader who takes the whole scene seriously, he'll somehow fit a rehearsal into that afternoon time once in a while. So if you do any of your own writing or practicing, you've got to snatch a few minutes here and fifteen minutes there. Man, that's like having a day job, like working in an office and trying to be yourself for a couple of hours at night.

"So"—Simmons drained another cup of coffee— "I took like a vow of poverty until and if I can get my own thing going."

"How do you eat?"

"Don't ask, man. I wait for accidents. Like I got three hundred sixty-six dollars for that album in September. That's the very least they could pay me. Just union scale. I'm still living on that. When things get down to nothing, I wash dishes or wait on tables. That keeps your mind free. I can be thinking my own music all the time I'm working, and when I've got enough bread together to pay the rent and buy some eggs for a while, I stop and I'm back in my own music full-time. So long as you don't get married, it's not that bad a scene."

I decided to walk Simmons home, and we went through the Village all the way across to Avenue B on the lower East Side. It was about five o'clock and the streets were full of kids, men on their way home, women doing last-minute shopping, and clusters of bums. Simmons lived in a rotting tenement even worse than Will Burke's building. His room was just as small as Burke's and had just about the same furniture except for a huge stack of old magazines on the bed. From what I could see quickly, they were of all kinds. *Negro Digest, Newsweek, Studies on the Left, Playboy, Partisan Review, Down Beat*. And some European magazines. One was opened to a picture of Simmons.

He followed my eyes and said, "Yeah, that was my trip to Elysium. Denmark has become *the* hip place in Europe. Hip enough, I mean, so that there's some kind of audience in Copenhagen for the 'new thing.' If you don't stay too long. A booker there got a copy of my album, the magazine wrote me up, and all of a sudden I had two weeks in Denmark. I didn't make much bread but, man—what it felt like to be able to play every night in front of an audience!"

Simmons stretched out on the bed, his hands behind his head, and stared at the ceiling. "You know what I found out?" He didn't wait for an answer. "How much energy I had. Everything was together. I was playing my own music and the music was making contact with people and I was like recharged every night so that during the day I functioned way above what I thought was my potential. I wrote and I practiced and I wrote again, and I was hardly ever tired. Those two weeks were worth a lot of dues."

"Here, though"—Simmons got up and began pacing, so far as he could pace in that tiny room— "it's like life and time have holes. I get tired, very tired, all of a sudden, not from working hard but from that extra effort of keeping myself going."

I began to wonder if Simmons ever had anybody to talk to. He hardly knew me, and yet there was no stopping him.

"I have to simulate life here. I mean, music is for getting to people. Playing at a loft once in a while or by myself doesn't make it. And not only that. The only way you really learn what you're doing and what you're not doing is by getting out there and feeling what gets across and what doesn't. When you're by yourself, you're never quite sure you're not conning yourself. Maybe the music you're making has no blood or bones. You don't know. You got nobody to bounce it off of. And how far *can* you simulate? Come on, come see my night club."

He picked up his trumpet case and we went down the stairs and into the cellar. The air was moist, and except for a small, naked light bulb over the broken furnace, the cellar was pitch black. "The super lets me come down here. I can't do it in the room. You play too loud and the guy upstairs starts banging on the floor, and the old lady next door begins to whimper. But here I can play as loud as I like. I used to try Central Park, but the fuzz there thought I was a nut and almost booked me for disturbing the peace. I was all alone on a hill and I couldn't see anybody anywhere—except the cop—and he said I was disturbing the peace. Then I tried what Sonny Rollins did the year he was away from the scene. I went up at night, high up on the Williamsburg Bridge, and just blew. It was great. It was like the whole city was my audience. But then one night, coming down off the bridge, I was mugged and they stole my horn. It took a lot of dirty dishes to pay for a new one, so that was the end of blowing in the wind."

Simmons was saying all this kind of calmly. He didn't sound especially bitter or sorry for himself. "How do you stand it?" I asked.

"Sometimes it is a drag." He took his horn out

of the case. "But I figure once you make up your mind where you want to go, you waste a lot of time if you brood about all the things you have to do—and do without—to get there. I'd rather save all the energy I can for the music. Besides, I'm still free. Broke, but free. Nobody tells me what to do. When I do get a job in a restaurant, I can always cut out if the guy's salty, because washing dishes or waiting on tables isn't my career, man."

"But what if you never make it? What if you never become famous?"

"You're talking like a kid. Famous!" Simmons snorted. "Sure, I'd like to be famous, but I put that away a long time ago. Your friend Godfrey is one of the last of *that* jazz line. He just got in under the wire. Where *we're* going, there ain't going to be any Louis Armstrongs or Duke Ellingtons or even Thelonious Monks. What I'm saying is that the old guys, like Louis and Duke, were showmen. They were also great musicians, but they made their bread because they could entertain a lot more people than actually dug what they were putting down. And Monk too in his way. I mean his audience is smaller, but because he's supposed to be an eccentric and he gets written up like that in *Time* and that sort of magazine, people come to see him. To see him, not so much to hear him. Godfrey too.

They figure he might make a speech at them, put them down. People *like* that. It puts some excitement into their lives. Or he might go into his dance. They don't know he does that to keep the rhythm straight. They figure he's a nut too.

"But us"—Simmons made a mock bow—"we're just musicians. Cecil, and George Russell, and the like. You come to hear us and all you get is the music, and there just ain't that many people willing to *concentrate*, to open *themselves* up to hear us. So where we're going is where the poets and the avant-garde classical composers have already been. Big bread we'll never make. Big magazines we'll never make. Only way I could get on the cover of *Time* is to shoot Lawrence Welk. And why bother? That cat has his groove. He's not bothering anybody."

Simmons picked up his horn and began to blow. It was the blues, but a strange blues. Again it was full of those human sounds—chuckles and burps and screams and scolding. But the beat was weird. I could feel some kind of pulse, but there was nothing in the music itself to pat your foot to right away. And the melody was like a ball of string that some magician had put a spell on. It unfolded and folded back on itself again and then went off in some wholly other direction and came back part way and then climbed up the wall and leapt to the other side of the room and then back into the horn.

I heard a rustle in the darkness. "The hippies are coming in for the early show," said Simmons. "Some rats are square and they only come around late when there's nothing else to do in the building. But a few of them show up as soon as I start. They're a great audience, man. They don't get drunk and they don't talk and they don't ask for requests."

I was feeling very uncomfortable. I'd seen a rat once, just once, when they were tearing down a building near where I live. It was big and brown and evil-looking. I didn't want to see another one, so I said I had to leave.

"O.K.," said Simmons. "Come back any time. No cover. No minimum. No age limit. This is the freest night club in the world." As I went up the stairs and into the front hall I could still hear the trumpet dimly. Maybe going to college for a while wasn't such a bad idea, after all.

13

The Offer

I was accepted at Amherst, and I told my parents I'd go. They were very pleased, but I was still torn up about whether I was doing the right thing or not. A couple of weeks after I got the letter, our band was in a contest at the Savoy on a Sunday afternoon. One of the big drum manufacturers ran a competition for amateur bands around the city. They got publicity out of it and the winning band won two hundred dollars along with a new set for its drummer. The judges were Art Blakey, Irving Weston, and George Dudley.

We were by no means the best band. There was a combo of hard-cookers from Bedford-Stuyvesant, a very slick band from Harlem, and a weird "new thing" group from the lower East Side. I still didn't understand the new jazz fully, but after the lessons with Hitchcock and the little I'd heard of Danny Simmons' trumpet, I was able to feel more in it than I had before. I had stopped worrying so much about exactly what they were doing with every note, and now just tried to react to the whole thing.

The hard-boppers from Bedford-Stuyvesant won, and we got an honorable mention which meant free subscriptions to *Down Beat* for all of us. We went over to the judges' table to give our names and addresses. "Think I can exchange this for a subscription to *The Liberator?*" Tim said to Weston. "It swings a lot more than *Down Beat.*" I'd seen *The Liberator.* It was a Negro nationalist magazine. It didn't seem to like *any* whites.

"All you'll learn from that is hate," Irving Weston said.

"I already learned"—Tim stared at him—"from reading you."

Weston looked shocked. "You don't know nothing, man," said Tim. "Yes, sir, jazz is a truly American art form. The critics make the money and the musicians scuffle."

"Now, see here—" Weston pointed his finger at Tim.

"You mess with me and you'll have to type with your nose." Tim walked away. Weston spluttered a bit, and the owner of the Savoy calmed him down with a free beer.

Dudley came over to me. I hadn't seen him since Christmas Day, but he made no mention of ever having met me before. He introduced himself, as if I wouldn't know who he was anyway, and motioned me to a table.

We sat down, and Dudley said, "How'd you like to turn pro?"

"Sure," I answered, Amherst flying out of my head.

"I'm making a change in the band," said Dudley. "Now let me be straight with you. You got a long way to go, a lot to learn, but I think that with some woodshedding you can get our book down. And I'll work with you as much as you need it. Now, I want you because you're good enough so you won't mess us up but mainly because you're also good publicity. You're a young unknown, your father is one of the biggest corporation lawyers in the country—"

"How did you know that?"

"I find out what I want to know. With you in the band, we could get some good publicity breaks at a time when we can use them. I'm going to shop around for some other record company to go with, and if I come to them after some national publicity, I can get more out of them. It'll also help in the clubs too. Well?"

"Uh—I think I want to. But can I let you know?" It had happened too fast, and besides, I just couldn't accept without at least letting my parents know about it in front.

"You're not likely to get a chance like this for a long time, if ever." Dudley was put out that I even hesitated. "Here's my number. You've got two days."

I was shaky when I got up. "What's happening?" Mike asked. He'd come down to cheer the band on. I told him and he whistled. "Wow! You going to take it?"

"I don't know." I saw Mary Hitchcock near the door. "Look,"—I moved away from Mike—"I want to go see Bill. See you later."

I asked Mary if Bill was home. "Yes, I'm going there now." And we started out. She didn't seem to want to talk, and maybe it was because we weren't talking that I became so conscious of the stares we were getting. Not everybody, but a lot of people would sort of look twice at us. Most would pretend not to, but you could see them sneak a glance. Even in the Village. That's what surprised me. You see a lot of mixed couples on the streets there, but these people were acting as if we were from Mars.

A matronly woman with white hair, and her husband, portly and red-faced, passed us on Eighth Street. "Well"—we heard her behind us—"that's exactly what you'd expect in the Village. Pretty soon the world's going to be full of mongrels."

Mary whirled around.

"Do ah bother you, missus?" She had put on a thick southern Negro accent.

The woman's mouth opened. "I beg your pardon?"

"Did ah shock you, missus"—Mary came closer to her—"walkin' along with dis nice white boy? Ah jus takin' care of him." She leaned closer and whispered, "He not right in de haid."

The woman didn't quite understand what was happening. She looked at me and I stared back at her, my mouth hanging, my eyes glazed. "I wanna ice cream," I whimpered. "I wanna choklit ice cream."

The husband, who seemed embarrassed and maybe did know what was going on, said to Mary, "I'm sorry if we offended you, miss."

"Aw, thass all right." Mary smiled. "All white folks ain't right in de haid. Lawdy, I sure worry who's gonna take care of dem when we stop."

The woman bit her lips, pulled her husband by the elbow, and marched away.

Mary smiled at me. "I bet," I said, "that lady would say—if you asked her—that she's not prejudiced."

"You're catching on, boy. You're catching on."

Bill was at the piano when we came in. Mary described what had happened. "Least you can do," said Bill, "is give him some chocolate ice cream." As Mary went into the kitchen, Bill went on, "Did you ever hear what happened to Moses and Veronica on Fifth Avenue?" I hadn't.

"It was a couple of years ago. They were walking by Tiffany's with Mary and me, and some starchy old cat whispered something salty to his wife as they walked by. Moses turned on them, popping his eyes and talking very crisply in the way Africans who were educated in British schools talk English. You know, it's like a cross between British and West Indian English. Well, he came on as the ambassador to the United Nations from Ghana and made as if the honor of his country had been attacked. He was going to bring the whole issue before the United Nations and he demanded their names and addresses.

"Man, you should have seen that old cat. First of all, I doubt if anybody had ever put him down before. Especially in public with the circle of people around us getting bigger and bigger as Moses roared on. And then, Moses was so damn convincing that when a cop came over, he began to look hard at the old cat, not at Moses. Well, the apologies flowed like syrup, and Moses finally, very haughty, said he might forget the incident. The old cat invited Moses and Veronica to dinner and Moses asked him if he'd ever had a black man to dinner before. The old cat mumbled that he hadn't and Moses said he didn't think he looked like a guinea pig and walked off."

Mary was back with the ice cream. "I got to tell

that other story," she said. Me, I was beaming. For the first time I felt part of the family. Almost, anyway. "You know Jenkins, that very dignified trombonist in Basie's band—the man with the almost white hair and that clipped moustache? He's about the blackest man I've ever seen and he carries himself very straight. The band had a week off last summer and Jenkins decided he wanted to see the United Nations. So I went along with him. In one of the corridors, one of those twittering white ladies came up to him and said, 'And how long have you been in the United States, sir?' She figured he was too dignified to be just any old, ordinary American black man. Jenkins looked at her as if she wasn't quite all there in the head and said, 'Fifty-two years, madam. I was born in Harlem.' "

We laughed and then I remembered why I was there. I told Bill about the offer from Dudley and asked his advice. He'd become somber, and when I was finished, he didn't say anything for a while.

"I don't know what to tell you," he began finally. "I don't think I *can* tell you anything. It bugs me."

"Why?" said Mary.

"There are plenty of Negro musicians who could use that job, that's why. Kids who don't have the option of going to college."

"But Tom didn't go *looking* for it." Mary was

disturbed. "Dudley came to *him*. Besides, I thought you were all for integration."

"That's not the point. What Dudley is doing isn't integration. It's exploitation. It won't hurt the kid but it does take a job away from a black man."

I hadn't even thought about that and I guess I looked as crushed as I felt. Here I'd felt accepted in their house for once, and all of a sudden, I'd been iced out again.

"That's a very rigid way of looking at it," Mary said.

"Why, Miss Mary," Bill answered sharply, "how you've changed. Used to be I was the one who wasn't nationalistic enough."

I didn't want to be in on any family arguments, so I got up and said good-bye. The atmosphere was very cool between them, and it was as if I wasn't there any longer before I even left.

The only thing I could figure to do now was ask Godfrey. I caught him outside the Savoy later that night.

"You want to do it?"

"I'm not sure. That's why I'm asking your opinion."

"Don't jive me. You must have a strong feeling one way or the other. What you're looking for now is a way to justify it."

"Yes, I want to. It's like dreaming of being a major leaguer all your life, and all of a sudden you get a chance to go with the Boston Red Sox. It's not the Yankees, but it's the big leagues."

Godfrey stroked his beard. "On the one hand," he said, "you know what I think of Dudley and his music. But it is experience and it is exposure. Now, for Danny Simmons to take that gig would be absolutely wrong. He's too far into his own thing now. But from what I've heard of you at Bill's, you're not. I still don't know, for that matter, whether you're *ever* going to have your own thing going. I just don't know. Sometimes I think you will, and sometimes I think you won't."

"You mean because I'm the wrong color."

Godfrey looked almost as mad as he had when he was talking to Irving Weston. "Boy, I thought you knew me. I don't care if a man is red all over with a purple nose and yellow eyes so long as he can play. You think Will Burke is passing or something? And he's not the first white man I've used. If I thought by color, I'd be just as locked in as most people are in this country."

"But what about Bill's point—that I'd be taking the job away from a Negro musician?"

"So did Burke when I hired him for that recording. Boy, this is no factory or bank. I see the sense

127

of going out and *looking* for Negroes if you're running a business that ain't had any before. But what is jazz all about if not *individuals?* Obviously, Dudley isn't thinking the way I am. He told you straight out why he wanted you. But he'd have done the same thing if Ralph Bunche's son played fair enough horn to make it in his band. Or Jackie Robinson's kid.

"There are two ways of thinking underneath color," Godfrey continued. "One is Dudley's— the money way. To a cat who's greedy, color gets forgotten if it's in the way of him making more bread. And the other way is just taking a man for what he is. If Bill ever told me I couldn't hire a white musician I *wanted*, Bill could go find another job."

"So what should I do?"

"I ain't finished. It makes no mind to me whether you go to college or you don't go. Some of the tightest squares I ever knew went to the *best* colleges. Some of the most *educated* men I know—men who know where it's at—didn't get through high school That's not what's bothering me. If you *are* serious about music, though, I just wonder whether it makes sense for you to *start* slick. It's too easy. You haven't begun to pay any dues. And I don't mean you have to live with rats to pay dues. I mean what does a guy know, for example, if he becomes a senator first time out? A guy who never ran for city council or state representative. What does a guy know who becomes a judge and has hardly ever been in a courtroom? I mean, what *kind* of senator or judge does he become that way?

"Like I said, Dudley isn't going to spoil your style, because you ain't got one yet. But he could make you forget how much you don't know, how little you have to say yet. I can see you a year from now running all over that horn and thinking you're a big man. You might even come up high in the polls, and your head would swell out like a pumpkin.

"That couldn't happen," I said.

"Oh, no? Fifteen years ago I knew a raggedy kid out of Chicago who used to come uptown to a place where me, Dizzy, and Bird jammed. This kid *begged* us to let him sit in, and once in a while we did. He was so humble he practically talked to you with his chin on his chest. He had something to say too, not much, but there was a little flame there. Two years later, he got a fluke record hit. And he was a big man ever after. Name of George Dudley." Godfrey almost spit out the last two words.

"So you don't think I ought to accept the offer?"

"Didn't say that. It's up to you, boy. You're old enough not to have to have somebody else make up your mind for you. Or give you reasons not to doubt your own reasons. What do your folks say?"

"I haven't told them yet. I want to be very sure in my own mind before I do."

"I don't understand you, boy. Why *are* you running around like this, asking everybody what you ought to do? You're coming on like a child."

For the first time I was angry at Godfrey. "Why," I almost yelled, "are grown-ups so damn sure of themselves when they see a younger person who isn't? Am I a child because I go to people I respect when I'm not sure what I ought to do? It isn't easy to decide. It just isn't. I don't know if I'm good enough to make it in the first place. I don't know if I'm strong enough not to get swallowed up by Dudley and what *he* thinks life is all about. Especially when I'm not so sure *I* know what it's all about."

"Cool it." Godfrey put his hand on my shoulder. "Look, boy, I can't make you sure of anything. You're right. It's not a simple decision. Like, it may be that going on the road—even with that mechanical man—may do you a lot of good. You've only seen a very small part of New York City, let alone America. A lot of the older cats put down the road, but I'm grateful for all the hard traveling I've done. I learned a lot about this country, about the rhythms of different parts of it, about different ways people

con themselves in different places while they think
they're conning you. When I get off the road after
a trip, boy, I don't need any Gallup poll or any
columnist to tell me what's going on. I *know*. More
I think about it, the more I'm convinced we ought to
travel a good deal more than we've been doing the
past couple of years. Everybody in the band's getting
too comfortable. Too settled."

Godfrey hadn't been any help and I walked east
toward Danny Simmons' place. It was a warm April
night and I was afraid Danny would be out somewhere. It was hard to imagine him being cooped up
on a night like this in that box of a room or that
gloomy cellar. He wasn't in his room, but as I
opened the cellar door I could hear the horn. A rat
ran over my foot, whizzing out the door, and I
yelled. Danny looked up and burst out laughing.

"Don't bug the customers, man." He waved.

I told him about my dilemma.

"I got nothing to say." He looked at me, his
trumpet resting against his chin. "To tell you the
truth, I can't put myself into you, so I can't figure
what the smart thing for you to do would be. No,
you got to play this one by yourself."

"What's going on down there?" A cop was standing inside the cellar door. "What was that yell?"

"Me," I said sheepishly. "A rat ran over my foot."

The cop came down. He had his billy out. "I said what's going *on* down here?"

"Everything's cool," Danny said softly. "We've just been talking."

"In a cellar? What are you holding?"

"Oh, man," Danny said in disgust, "we're not junkies. We're musicians, man."

"Same thing," the cop snapped. "Up—against the wall."

"Hey," I said, "you can't search us just like that. We haven't done anything. You're infringing on our civil liberties. My father's a lawyer—" The billy hit me in the stomach and I doubled over.

"That's one for civil liberties," said the cop. "You got any other advice for me?"

"Cool it, cool it," Danny whispered.

The cop searched us, and I mean searched. The only person who's ever given me a going over like that is our family doctor for the annual checkup. But this cop had no doctor's touch. He used his hand as if it were a claw hammer.

"You guys are pretty cute," he said. "Where did you stash it?"

"Officer," Danny spoke slowly, politely, "we do not have any drugs. We do not have any marijuana. You are welcome to come up to my room to look. I am not hiding a thing."

The cop looked suspiciously at Danny and then
at me. "Ah, I probably couldn't find it anyway in
here. I'll let you off this time, but stay out of this
cellar."

"Is it illegal—" I began, and Danny nudged me
hard.

"Something *else?*" The cop raised the billy.

"No, sorry," I said. We went up the stairs, the cop
behind us. Outside, we went one way and he went
the other.

"That's awful." I was furious. "He treated us like
we had no rights at all."

Danny laughed. "He thought you lived down
here, man. If he'd found you in a cellar where *you*
live, he would have been smooth as glass. He'd figure
your old man might have some pull and might get
him busted if he got out of line. But with us, he
doesn't have a thing to worry about."

"Something ought to be done."

"That's right. But I ain't about to do it. You need
politics to change that scene, man. You need guys
in office who wouldn't stand for this kind of jive. But
there's nothing a musician can do about *that.*
Maybe you ought to think about that."

"What do you mean?"

"Well, unless you're something really special on
that horn—and I'm not saying you might not be

someday—you could maybe be important in some other way. I don't mean just important to yourself, but to a lot of other people. I mean if that's the route you wanted to take. There's a kid in this building. A real bright Puerto Rican kid. I talked him deaf for months. He was going to quit school so he could make a lousy sixty dollars a week in the garment district. But I *knew* that boy had a good mind. And he's a leader. He's got that thing, whatever it is. The other kids around here listen to him. So I kept telling him to go on to college. With what he learned there, maybe he could get some power and help straighten out this kind of scene."

"You saying I ought to become like a crusader?"

"I don't know you that well, man. For all I know, maybe you got a picture of Hitler over your bed. But I do know you're smart and you talk good. I'm just saying maybe you could swing better in something else than jazz. I'm not that square I think music is the only worthwhile scene. It is for *me,* but I have other heroes than Monk and Ornette Coleman."

"Like who?"

"Like William Douglas and some of those cats on the Supreme Court. They swing. Like Robert Moses, that civil rights guy in Mississippi. He knows where it's at."

"Well, I still don't know what to do."

"I'm going up, man. Talking with a cop tires me out. Whatever you do, send me a postcard, man."

"Danny, do you really think I have any potential on the trumpet?"

"If I had a strong answer to that for myself, I'd feel a lot better than I do. If you're looking for a sign from somewhere or somebody, you'll go lame looking." He went up the stairs. "Later." He waved, and went inside.

14
Late Blues

I walked back to the Village from Danny's place. It was nearly midnight, and I was no clearer about what I should do than when I'd started. On an impulse, I went to Veronica's and knocked.

The music was going—a new Afro-Cuban album by Dizzy—and Veronica was alone. She took the record off, motioned me to a seat, and waited for me to begin. One of the things I like about Veronica is that you don't need any preliminaries with her. She figured that at that time of night I hadn't come for small talk.

I told her about Dudley's offer and the reactions I'd been getting from Hitchcock, Godfrey, and Danny Simmons.

"Another thing," I went on, "is that I'm afraid of losing jazz if I don't go with it all the way now. I mean, in a few years I'd be out of it. I wouldn't know everything that was happening *as* it happened, I'd miss up on more and more albums, and finally, I'd be like my father who talks of being a Benny Goodman fan way back when but hasn't played any of his swing records for years and years."

"That needn't happen," Veronica said. "Let's

not confuse two different things. Your main hang-up is whether you want to be a musician full-time *now*. What you just talked about is something else. As for that first thing, no one can really help you. No one can take a bath for you, no one can eat for you, no one can die for you. And no one can decide your life's work for you. What I don't share is your sense of urgency about making this decision—whether to go with Dudley—the crucial one. You're so young. If you did try college for a year or two, and kept playing while you were there, you'd still be able to drop out, if that's how you felt, and come back here to try to make it in jazz."

"Maybe"—it had just occurred to me—"I'm afraid that I might like college well enough to stay."

Veronica laughed. "You can't have *everything*. Well, suppose you do like college that well. That leads to your second worry—that jazz would rush past you, that you'd be out of it. Do you think *I'm* that square?"

I looked around at all the records and remembered how impressed I'd been the first time there at how inside she was. "No," I said, "but you've got all that time to keep up. I'd be studying and eventually working at something else, and it would be like losing a valuable part of me. Maybe the most valuable."

"You really think I just sit here all day and play records? Jessica must have told you I paint, but with her charming delight in understatement, she probably didn't tell you that I spend more hours a week on painting than most men work. And I sell them too! At pretty stiff prices, young man. So I'm not the ancient, slothful hippie you think me. If you haven't been kidding yourself and if jazz really does mean that much to you, it will keep *on* meaning that much and you'll *make* time for it. If you do fall behind, that'll mean either its roots in you weren't as deep as you thought, or you've changed."

"That's what I'm worried about basically," I said, "—changing."

"Well, I hope you don't intend to stay seventeen all your life. A swinging Peter Pan. You mean you don't want to lose what drives you now—the passion, the seriousness. Yes, there is a terrible danger that as people grow older, they lose the conviction that there are enormously important things to be done and to be experienced. But if you think holding on to jazz like a security blanket is going to keep you young, you're a fool. With or without jazz, you'll either grow up or—like most people—you'll grow sideways."

As I was mulling over what she'd said, Godfrey came in. He was scowling and for the first time since

I'd known him, he was very nervous. He kept tugging at his beard and he kept biting his lips. He ignored me and rushed up to Veronica.

"You got any bread handy? Enough for a thousand dollar bail bond?"

"Sure." Veronica got up.

"Danny. Danny Simmons. They just busted him. They busted him *up.*"

"Where? What did he do?" Veronica asked.

"What does that cat ever do? He was playing music, bothering nobody. In that cellar he hangs out in."

Danny went back downstairs, I thought, and so did that cop.

"A cop hauled him out of there," Godfrey went on, "for disturbing the peace. Ain't that something! And because Danny didn't move fast enough, the cop disturbed his face. Right on the chops. That boy isn't going to be able to blow anything for weeks."

Veronica had taken some money out of a book in the bookcase and gave it to Godfrey. "If he wants, Moses, bring him here. He can stay as long as he likes."

"Disturbing the peace," Godfrey was mumbling as he went out the door. "The peace of this city *should* be disturbed."

I told Veronica about what had happened earlier

in the cellar and then we fell into silence, "Maybe,"
I blurted out, "I could go out with Dudley for six
months, and enter college late."

"Tommy." Veronica rose, clearly irritated. "Your
problems simply aren't that big. I know they seem
big to you, but they just aren't."

I was hurt and I said very stiffly that I guessed
I'd been keeping her up and I'd be leaving now.
She saw me to the door and put her hand on my
shoulder as I started downstairs. "This last year has
been a kind of trial for you, hasn't it? Trying to
make it through the racial looking glass. Trying to
make it in jazz. Trying to make it as a man. It's the
kind of trial that can drive you crazy. Because you're
also the judge, the jury, the prosecutor, and the
defense attorney. All the rest of us are just witnesses.
And we're you too, for that matter, because we exist
and react as you think we do. And right now you
think we're putting you down.

"I don't imagine you realize that Moses and Bill
wouldn't have you around as much as they do if
they weren't fond of you. He'd be angry if I told
you, but Moses said one night—only three-quarters
kidding—that he wished he could adopt you.
You've been trying very hard, Tom, to be, and
not just exist. I don't think you're going to lose that
thing. Some people are middle-aged by the time

they're ten. And some people never stop swinging until they stop, period. I think you may be in that honored company, young man. And it really doesn't have that much to do with how you play that horn of yours. I'll dig you even if you don't ever make a record."

She kissed me on the cheek and went inside. I felt like I'd been crowned or something, but I sure didn't have any kingdom. I felt good though. Until I remembered Danny.

15
Open End

So I'm at Amherst. I can't tell you just when I decided to try college for a while. I do remember exactly when I made up my mind not to go with Dudley. It just hit me clearly walking home from Veronica's that night. Since I didn't like him, I couldn't play with him. I mean, if you're in a man's band, you have to be talking to him in the music, and there was nothing I had to say to him—except "I don't want to be like you."

With that decided, I guess I gradually figured I had time to try some alternatives. After all, I'm not locked in here. I can split in a year or two if I want to. And the scene isn't too bad. We have a combo going at the school and I sometimes jam in Springfield and Worcester. Twice I've been to Boston and sat in there. And between us my roommate and I keep up on the new records. So it's not as if I'm totally isolated.

And last week Godfrey came through on a college concert tour. I sure was a big man here then. He came up to the room, he kept telling people I was a protégé of his, and he even dedicated a number to me at the concert.

The only thing that hurt at the concert was seeing Danny Simmons with Godfrey. I mean I was glad his mouth had healed and that Godfrey had decided to enlarge his group and hire Danny. But I kept thinking, "It should have been *me* up there." But as I listened, I knew it couldn't be. It's not only that Danny is so much better than I am, but he's so much his own man on that horn. He really had become a kind of co-leader with Godfrey. They did as many of Danny's tunes as Godfrey's, and Danny had actually managed to make it in that band without losing his own thing. It was as if Godfrey had opened up the music to make room for him. The only other change in the band was a new bass player. Bill had decided to stay in New York to free-lance and study composition.

After the concert, I showed Danny around the campus.

"It's sure peaceful here," he said. "And cool. It's no wonder some guys become professors. This kind of place is like one of the last refuges from all that rushing and cheating and biting out there."

"It's not heaven," I said. "There's a lot of pettiness here too."

"Yeah," said Danny, "but it's like protected here. I don't mean this is a scene for me. I made my decision a long time ago. I'm doing what I want to do.

I didn't even mind that thirty days in jail too much."

"Thirty days?"

"Yeah. Remember? I was disturbing the peace. But it wasn't so bad. I talked to a lot of different cats, and hearing their stories got me out of myself. If I'd been on the outside, not being able to play until my chops healed, I'd probably have brooded the time away. You know who was in with me? Fred Godfrey. No jive. He'd been in a peace demonstration. He laid down right in the middle of Times Square protesting the war in South Vietnam. He got thirty days too. He's still eating at himself, though. He was saying he had to do *this* kind of protest because just protesting against Jim Crow is too narrow. 'What if we get integrated into a society that's going to blow itself up?' he said. I told him he didn't have to convince *me* of anything. It was cool with me whether he protested or didn't." Danny paused. "It's a funny thing," he finally said. "It's getting so almost everybody I know is an ex-con."

"I haven't been in jail," I said glumly.

"Don't despair, man. You may get lucky."

I walked Danny to the band bus, a Volkswagen Godfrey had bought when he decided to start going on long tours again. Sam Mitchell was stretched on a seat. He waved at me limply and grimaced. "You're smart, boy. You stay in the same bed every night. Me, I'm turning into a road map. These ain't lines in my face. They're routes."

"How you spelling that?" Godfrey came up behind us.

"Without the double 'o,' daddy," said Mitchell.

"Yeah, I read you all right. Those routes all lead to New York, but we're not going to be back there for a long time."

"I know," said Sam. "I'm serving my time before I get to heaven. And when I die"—he spread his hands—"I'm going to walk right into a pad full of all the latest conveniences, and I'll never walk out again."

"That's exactly what's going to happen, Sam." Godfrey laughed. "Exactly." He held out his hand to me. "Boy, don't lose touch. I want to see what happens to you. O.K.," he shouted, "everybody in!"

"Don't blow your cool." Danny shook hands with me. "But don't be too cool. Later."

Two days later, I got a postcard from New York:

Dear Tom—
Moses says you're making it. Keep cooking. And next time you're back, come by for some choklit ice cream.

                              Miss Mary and Bill

I'm still not absolutely sure I'm going to stay here at Amherst. I may quit any time and try to get a gig playing back home. But I'll probably stay at least until the end of the next year. There's a guy teaching sociology who really cooks, and I can take his course next year. He's very strong on getting people in neighborhoods like Danny's to organize *themselves* to change things. I still remember that cop in the cellar and I wonder what that sociology cat has to say about changing *that* scene. But, much as I'm looking forward to his course, there are nights when I'd give anything to be in that Volkswagen with Godfrey. After all, I could take one year off somewhere along the line. Couldn't I?

Nat Hentoff is a native of Boston, Massachusetts. He is a graduate of Northeastern University, did postgraduate work at Harvard, and studied at the Sorbonne on a Fulbright fellowship. Now a staff writer for *The New Yorker,* he makes his home in New York City.

Mr. Hentoff is a frequent lecturer on jazz and the originator of a number of well-known jazz programs on radio in Boston and New York. Onetime associate editor of *Down Beat* magazine and co-editor of *The Jazz Review,* he is also the author of THE JAZZ LIFE, PEACE AGITATOR, and THE NEW EQUALITY. JAZZ COUNTRY is his first novel for young readers.